THE BRIDE'S BROTHER

AN INDIAN BILLIONAIRE ROMANCE

P. G. VAN

Copyright © P. G. Van
All Rights Reserved.

This book has been published with all efforts taken to make the material error-free after the consent of the author. However, the author and the publisher do not assume and hereby disclaim any liability to any party for any loss, damage, or disruption caused by errors or omissions, whether such errors or omissions result from negligence, accident, or any other cause.

While every effort has been made to avoid any mistake or omission, this publication is being sold on the condition and understanding that neither the author nor the publishers or printers would be liable in any manner to any person by reason of any mistake or omission in this publication or for any action taken or omitted to be taken or advice rendered or accepted on the basis of this work. For any defect in printing or binding the publishers will be liable only to replace the defective copy by another copy of this work then available.

Contents

Contents

1

Seema's dark almond eyes took in the beauty of the outdoor space set up with flowers and candles combined with beautiful and flowing silk fabric for the engagement party. It was a beautiful evening, and the breeze slightly eased her anxiety that had built up as they got closer to the time when the guests were about to arrive.

She and her small yet mighty team had handled many weddings the past few years since she started her business but none to this scale nor the type of events that needed unique themes and setup. This would be one of the first weddings that constituted more pre-wedding events, including a major weekend wedding planned two months after the engagement party.

Seema let out a deep breath, relieved that she could meet her client, Riya's requests for the evening but knew the real challenges were still to come. Riya was a young interior designer who had a unique requirement for her wedding unlike any other client Seema had worked with, which only excited her further, although it was also nerve-wracking.

"Seema, Mr. Vasudev is looking for you." Nandu, her best friend, roommate, and her production manager, said into her earpiece.

"Oh," Seema looked around and found Riya's father in deep conversation with his mother. "I see him, he is talking to Riya's grandmother. I will check in with him once they are done conversing."

She heard Nandu giggle. "The younger, Mr. Vasudev, Riya's brother, and he is not a happy camper."

Seema turned to scan the small group of family members who were gathered at the event. "I don't see him. Where is he?"

"Seema?" A deep male voice came from behind, and she turned around. She lifted her chin, and her eyes met the deep brown eyes of the tall man who stood in front of her. His eyes matched Riya's, and she knew he had to be her brother.

"Hello, Mr. Vasudev. Nice to meet you." She held out her hand, and there was a moment of hesitation before he reached out to take her hand in his.

"Raghav." His tone was curt.

"How can I help, sir?"

"What is going on?" His question threw Seema off, but it would not be the first time a client was asking such a question.

"Sir, is everything okay?" She looked around the space wondering if something was wrong.

"No. It's not. Your job is to make sure the events run smoothly but not at the cost of Riya feeling stressed about her outfit to the point she has tears in her eyes."

"Oh... I'm sorry, sir, but Riya was the one who had chosen the outfit to wear tonight."

"And you told her she could not change the outfit?" He sounded pissed.

She took a deep breath. "Sir, it was the arrangement we made according to Riya's requirements. She wanted the silk fabric we used for the décor to compliment her dress, and the artwork on the tablecloth to match her outfit. She also wanted an element of her outfit to be a part of her close family's outfits, including your tie. Changing her outfit would have a cascading set of changes."

He looked down at his tie for a moment, then looked at Seema. "I don't care. You will do what Riya wants going forward. She doesn't need to go through this stress."

"Sir, I understand, but Riya had set aside three dresses we could have managed with the décor if she had chosen any one of them, but she wanted a completely different palette of colors, and there was no way we could change everything at the last minute."

He looked at her for a long moment. "I don't care what it takes. Make sure you don't stress her out again like this. Even if it means you need to change everything and double the size of the people working, do it."

Seema shook her head. "I'm sorry I can't do that, Mr. Vasudev. Riya's main requirement was that we be as eco-friendly as possible, so we can't rip off the decor we build and randomly hire just anyone to take care of the event. Every piece of the décor is custom and handmade, and we will reuse the fabric and props for her other events."

"I don't care. Do whatever you need to do, so my sister doesn't have to feel the way she did this evening," he fumed.

Seema knew not to push further. "Sure, sir."

She let out a sigh of relief when he turned away from her, glad that she dodged that bullet without having to reveal the real reason why her client was upset.

The overwhelming feeling from the huge change in her life brought tears to her client's eyes, and she was not going to tell anyone, not even to the protective bride's brother, what her client shared in confidence.

"What was that about? He seemed to have burned you with his glare." Nandu's giggle came through the earpiece.

"Nothing. Watch the caterers. Make sure the drinks and food are served at the right temperature."

"Yes, ma'am." Nandu laughed.

Seema made one final check on all the other areas of the event before walking toward the suite where Riya was hanging out with her cousins while she waited for her future fiancé's family to arrive. She heard Riya's laugher as she got closer to the entrance of the suite and stopped short when she saw her brother standing by the doorway, speaking on the phone.

He looked up, and Nandu was right. The man still looked so pissed, he could burn her to the ground with his glare. She walked past him and went up to Riya from behind and gently tapped on her shoulder. "All okay? Ready for your party?"

Riya let out a squeal of joy and turned around to hug Seema. "Yes, I'm so happy." She pulled back and whispered, "Thank you for being there for me... you know."

"My pleasure, Riya. Deepak and his family are on their way and should arrive in the next ten minutes."

"Thank you, Seema. I hope Raghav was not too mean to you. He stormed out after hearing my cousin tell him I was stressed over my dress before even I could tell him anything else."

"Not a problem, ma'am."

"Hey, didn't we agree that you would call me Riya?" The young woman laughed.

"Yes. I can't believe you added that to the contract." Seema smiled.

"I knew that was the only way." Riya laughed and added, "Thank you for taking the blame for—"

"No problem. Are you ready to get engaged?"

"Now I am." Riya winked.

A few hours later, Seema looked around the crowded outdoor space and let out a sigh of relief knowing the event was going on without a hitch.

"Incoming," Nandu said into Seema's earpiece.

"Now what?"

"The young Mr. Vasudev is headed your way, again."

"What happened?" Seema looked around the space but could not see him, and as if on instinct, she turned around to find him walking toward her, not looking too thrilled.

"I have no idea," she heard Nandu say, and Seema pasted a smile on her face as Riya's brother approached her.

"Okay, I will talk to him," she said into the earpiece before asking, "Hello, sir. How can I help?"

He looked at her for a long moment. "I would like your help to find another wedding planner for my sister's wedding."

She took a deep breath telling herself not to lose her cool or be intimidated by the man who was being vocal about his dissatisfaction. "I don't think I can help you there because I am the planner for Riya Vasudev's wedding."

"Is this some kind of a joke for you?"

"Sir, with all due respect, my team and I take our job very seriously."

He looked at her like she just told him the biggest lie. "You are joking, right? You call the crew running the kitchen a serious bunch? They have never worked on a menu of this kind nor have the experience catering to a group this size."

She nodded. "I am aware, sir, and by the way the engagement party is going on, I see no problem with the caterers."

"What if there was an issue? What if they messed up? You chose someone who has no experience cooking for such events."

"Now they do."

Those words seemed to rub him the wrong way. "You listen to me, Seema. My sister's wedding is very important to our family, and I cannot let any of the events go wrong and upset her. I only want people who are experienced and not someone who will use my family events as their test ground."

"But, sir, that is how we keep our costs low while offering—"

"Who said you need to keep the cost low? Hire the best. There are no limits on the budget. This is my sister's wedding." He was aggravated but, she maintained her composure.

"With all due respect, sir, Riya chose my team and me to handle her wedding because of our unique business model. While keeping the cost low, I always look for ways to give a budding business a chance to shine, and it makes every aspect of the event different."

"Do you even understand what I am saying?"

She nodded. "Riya chose me because she believes in promoting new businesses. That's an idea we connected on and my business model. I cannot change it."

"Well, I guess it's time for me to change the wedding planner, then," he challenged.

Seema was about to lose her cool, but she stayed calm. "Sir, I understand you want the best for your sister, but this is what she chose. My business model is unique, and that's why she decided to work with me."

"Unique? It's ridiculous because no one runs a business with so much risk." He snickered.

"Please be assured that we have all the required backup plans to address unexpected problems," she stated confidently.

"Really?"

"Yes, sir."

He narrowed his eyes at her before reaching into his pocket to hand her a business card. "Call my assistant and make an appointment. I want to review this so-called backup plan you have for every one of the events that are planned for the next few weeks."

She took the card from him. "Absolutely, Mr. Vasudev."

"And the name is Raghav," he almost spat.

"Sure, Raghav sir. I will make an appointment. Please enjoy the rest of the evening."

"I am going to try."

With those famous words, he walked away from her. She stood looking at him wondering why he was so worked up about how things were set up.

Did something go wrong?

Whatever the case, she knew the man would be watching everything her team did going forward, and she had to ensure everything went according to plan. However annoyed she was, there was no ignoring the fact that he was being a protective brother. Too bad she had to deal with his grouchy side.

"Oh man, I'm so glad I didn't have to deal with him," Nandu grumbled as they started closing down the event after the last guest left.

"He is a concerned brother and a client. We need to stay calm," Seema maintained a stern tone.

"He sounded like a monster when he found those kids clicking pictures of the actress."

"Nandu, they were supposed to surrender their phones."

Nandu rolled her eyes. "They did. One of the kids from the culinary school is into photography and had a real camera in their backpack."

"Make sure this doesn't happen again."

"It's not like the actress didn't want to take pictures, she was even posing for them."

Seema shook her head. "Rules are rules, Nandu."

"Whatever. We have dealt with so many tough clients but never the client's brother," Nandu said and started laughing.

"What's so funny?" Seema asked as she checked the status update from all the areas of the event on her phone.

"Riya's brother is Brozilla like Bridezilla. Get it?"

"No making jokes on clients." Seema shook her head, but as she walked away, she couldn't help but smile.

Brozilla. The Bride's Brother.

2

Seema handed the car keys to the valet attendant as she stepped out of the car in front of Raghav's office building. It had been three days since the engagement party, and she spent some extra time to present the plan and logistics for the upcoming events to Riya's brother. He didn't care about the party themes or the type of party, he just wanted to ensure the guests were treated well and things didn't go wrong when it came to the food and entertainment.

At first, she was annoyed that she had to explain everything again, but she knew it wouldn't hurt to explain it to get him off her back. Maybe, he will let her manage the events the way they were planned if she answered all his questions and addressed his concerns.

She followed the instructions to his office located on the top floor and stepped out of the elevator when it stopped. The doors opened to an open area that was as big as the one in the lobby, and the glass walls offered a beautiful view of the city as the sun set over the hills at a distance.

"The view is amazing at this time of the day," the voice of a woman brought her eyes to the large, circular desk that was set to one side of the lobby. "You must be Seema."

Seema smiled at the older lady, probably in her fifties, as she approached the desk. "Yes, and I'm here to see Mr. Vasudev."

The older lady let out a laugh. "Don't call him that, sweetheart. He is not a fan of the formal way of addressing people. You can call him by his first name. He prefers that."

And I prefer to call him Mr. Vasudev, even if it annoys him.

Seema bit back a smile and said, "I will remember that."

"Can I get you something to drink? Raghav should be done with his meeting shortly."

"Thank you for asking. I'm fine." Seema sat on one of the chairs that gave her the best view of the city. As she looked at the tall buildings, her thoughts went back to her search to find her family. A connection her instincts told her she had out there, but she had not been successful in finding them the last couple of years even after hiring multiple private investigators.

She grew up in an orphanage in a different state and had moved to this city for work, but she longed to go back to the area where she grew up in hopes of finding a relative if someone was out there.

Seema looked up when a door to her right opened, and her eyes met the dark brown ones of the man she wasn't looking forward to conversing with but needed to get it over with. She knew the areas where he would have concerns with her plan, and she came prepared, or so she hoped.

She was surprised when he gave her a nod and said, "I'm sorry to keep you waiting, but I will need a few more minutes."

"Not a problem, Mr. Vasudev," she said it out of habit and saw the look of disappointment in his eyes that triggered a thrill inside her, a cheap one. She realized how much he disliked being addressed formally.

He handed the woman behind the desk an envelope and said, "Please make sure this gets to Singapore tomorrow."

The older woman nodded. "Consider it done. And I left all the details for your meetings tomorrow on your desk."

"Kamala ma'am, enjoy your days off." He chuckled and then turned to look at Seema. "I will be ready to meet in five minutes."

Seema nodded and looked at the older woman who was looking at her disapprovingly. "You need to stop calling him Mr. Vasudev. He doesn't like formalities."

Seema smiled. "Did I just hear him address you as *ma'am?*"

The older woman let out a laugh. "It's an old habit. You must know that I was his teacher in high school, and he chose to call me Kamala ma'am instead of Mrs. Sharma like he did back then."

"Good to know." Seema wanted to know why the elderly woman chose to give up teaching to work for her student, but she didn't want to start the conversation. How much she loved to hear such stories, she knew she couldn't start the conversation when she had no time.

"Seema," the older woman said a couple of minutes later, making her look up from her phone. "He is ready for you."

"Thank you, Mrs. Sharma. So nice to meet you."

"Same here, darling. I can tell you and Raghav will get along very well," the older woman mocked.

Seema opened the door and stepped into his office.

"Please come in, Ms. Kumar." His tone was flat.

Did he just call me Ms. Kumar?

"Thank you, sir." She smiled when he gestured for her to take one of the chairs set to one side of the office, away from his desk.

"You are welcome, madam." He nodded. "Please tell me you have hired professionals for all the upcoming events."

Why is he being so weird and formal? Payback? Sure, let's play.

"With all due respect, sir, everyone we hired for the engagement event are all professionals."

He looked at her in silence for a moment. "My apologies, madam. What I am looking for is an experienced and professional team. Not the group of kids plating the food that was being served to dignitaries and celebrities who will be attending the events."

The way he said 'madam' was getting on her nerves. He was twisting the word and making it sound weird, and his opinion about the team she had chosen for the engagement party further fueled her annoyance. "As far as I know, my team only got compliments from our client for their effort."

"That's because nothing went wrong. What if something blew up because of their inexperience?"

"Rest assured, we have it all covered."

"Give me an example." He was becoming impatient, and Seema knew no matter what she told him about Plan B or Plan C, it would not appease him. She had to understand what triggered the concern.

"Sir, we have a limited amount of time, and I will not be able to cover the details of every aspect of the event. I'm happy to share the project plan we used to execute the event. So, I request that you let me know what it is that you were unhappy about at the event."

He thought for a moment and said, "In fact, I might have something that I could show you."

She shifted nervously when he walked over to his desk to pick up his phone and swiped through like he was looking for something specific. He walked back to her and held his phone screen in front of her. The image on the screen showed the engaged couple holding hands, standing under a beautiful marble arch decorated with flowers, while the young photographer lay on his back, between the couple's feet trying to capture a one-of-a-kind picture while two other men leaned over from tall ladders, one spraying water to create the effect of mist and another man holding a white light. The picture of the couple surrounded by the technicians looked funny, but they were doing their job.

"Do you even realize how hazardous it could be with these types of stunts. What if one of the guys fell and got hurt or worse, they fell on Riya or Deepak?"

Seema nodded as she pulled out her phone and handed it to him. "Please look at this wallpaper I have on my phone. This is the picture that was taken with those stunts."

Seema bit her lip to stop from smiling when she saw his eyes widen, just like hers had when she saw the picture of the happy couple. The picture was a masterpiece, and it looked like the couple was surrounded by mini rainbows from the light shining through the water droplets from the mist spray.

"That, sir, is what Riya wanted. A unique set of pictures, a new way of experiencing her wedding, and beautiful memories created with every event, and she chose my team out of thirty other event-planning companies that auditioned for the project."

He kept his eyes on her phone screen like he could not believe the picture he was looking at. Seema saw how much the bride's brother adored his little sister, but that was gone in a flash as he handed her phone back to her. "You lucked out at the event. It was a miracle there weren't a series of disasters that happened that day. I need you to change the team you hired and get experienced people to work with you."

"If you are going to replace the people I hire, you might as well replace me, sir."

He pursed his lips, and she saw a flicker of disbelief in his eyes. "Ms. Seema Kumar, my sister wants everything to be unique, and that's who she is, but I can't let the most important event in her life be ruined by your callousness to prove your business model."

"It's not just about my business model, sir."

"What is it then? Is there a cheap thrill in hiring folks who have no clue what they are doing and hope nothing goes wrong?" he almost spat.

"That's not it. It's about bringing in fresh ideas. Like I said, that was one of the reasons I was hired for the job."

He took in a deep breath like he was trying to calm himself down. "Fine. This is what I want. I want to review the plan for every one of the events set up at least two weeks prior. I will have a lot of questions, and you better have answers for all of them."

Brozilla. He suits the name perfectly.

"Sure, sir."

"Ms. Seema Kumar, I prefer a business-casual approach, but if you insist that we keep the formalities, then I guess I will have to be formal, too."

"Thank you for understanding."

He nodded. "How is it that you are not formal with Riya?"

She smiled, remembering the condition her client included in the contract. "It was an item she added in the agreement."

He let out a laugh, pride filling his eyes. "That's my sister."

"Riya is a good and reasonable client."

"And I ask that you don't take advantage of her flexibility. I want everything she hopes for to happen, not just for the events but in her life."

"Absolutely, sir." An idea popped in her head, and she knew it was the right time to ask him for the impossible. "Riya did mention that her cousins wanted to work on a dance performance for the Sangeet, and her hope was that you would dance as well."

"What?" He shook his head. "Not happening."

Seema knew her client would be thrilled if she got her brother to participate. "Sir, I agreed to work with you to address your concerns, and all I ask is that you participate in the dance performance with your family."

"No. I know how much Riya would love for me to dance with the family, but I can't... even if I could dance, my schedule would not allow it."

Seema thought for a moment. "How about you keep this a complete surprise? You can practice with one of our choreographers and join in as a surprise."

"Not happening."

She fell silent with how adamant he sounded. "Sir, please think about how surprised Riya will be if you were to dance."

Something flickered in his eyes, and she hoped he would agree, but he didn't budge. "Ms. Seema Kumar, why don't we focus on the upcoming events and think about the dance later?"

"Sure, sir."

"Can you please stop with the *sir*? I think I prefer Mr. Vasudev if you must be formal." He rolled his eyes.

"Sounds good, Mr. Vasudev."

"Please set up a time for a weekly meeting, and we can have the review online. You don't need to drive all the way here for the meetings. We can use technology."

"Thank you, sir."

"Can we review the plan for all the events?"

"Sure." She handed him the portfolio and waited for him to look through the logistic details.

"What is the taste test?" He pointed at one of the line items on a calendar.

"That's when we have the potential vendors prepare a platter for our clients, so we can choose the right team for the event."

"Who did the taste test for the food served at the engagement party?"

"Riya and Mr. and Mrs. Vasudev."

He nodded like he was comfortable with the idea. "How do you make sure the vendor you chose knows how to handle the event?"

"Our vendor selection process is very rigorous. We pick upcoming but good vendors to assess. The assessment considers customer reviews and other online feedback, and we also do an on-site assessment.

"On-site?"

"Yes, for example, either someone on my team or I spend an entire day in the restaurant kitchens on their busiest days to make sure they can handle the volume for an event and also any unexpected situations gracefully."

"Did you not assess the culinary students before hiring them for the party?"

"Mr. Vasudev, the culinary students were on a break and were having some fun. I don't understand what was so alarming that you found them chatting and laughing."

"They were there on a job, and they weren't there to discuss our guests."

Seema nodded. "I agree. And you must know we only chose the students with the best conduct, and they were only admiring Riya's friend who is a famous actress."

"Not acceptable going forward. Also, no pictures or videos to be taken by anyone other than the designated person at any of the events."

"Privacy of our client is of utmost importance, and we have a policy that the staff cannot carry their personal devices."

"Okay, but remember I will not tolerate something like this again," he issued a warning.

"You are overreacting, Mr. Vasudev."

His eyes narrowed, and she knew he did not like the words nor the tone. "Then you better take care of such matters."

"Thank you for your input. I will send the details of each event as soon as I have them, and we can talk if you have questions." She stood up before she said something that would make the conversation go sideways and left his office without another look in his direction.

Seema knew it was abrupt for her to leave in that manner, but she knew he had asked her the questions he had, and there was nothing else she could provide for him to suddenly feel confident about her team's capabilities.

She decided to take on the challenges as they occurred, even if it was in the form of an annoyed bride's brother.

Chapter 3

"Did Riya finalize her outfit for the wedding and reception? Do we have the décor plan drafted?" Seema asked, looking at her team during their Friday morning meeting.

Nandu shook her head. "She says she is not set on a dress yet."

Seema let out a sigh. "Can we get the designers to give us the details of the outfits, so we can plan for the props and decoration? They can work with Riya on the style."

"That's a negative, Seema. Riya is yet to like a dress that she wants to wear for the reception and other events." Nandu sounded frustrated.

"What about the wedding saree? That should be set because I know Riya's mother had chosen that for her."

"Nope. Riya confirmed she will not be wearing one of those sarees. She wants the designer to make her a custom saree with the traditional silk."

Seema thought for a moment. "Have Neeraj get in touch with Riya. If she has not liked any of the designers' outfits, she is not going to find anything she likes."

"Neeraj is not in the same league as the designers Riya has been working with. Are you sure he can meet her requirements?" Nandu speculated.

"We shall see. She may or may not, but we need to change the strategy."

Nandu nodded, and Seema turned her attention to Jai, her entertainment lead. "How is the performance prep coming along?"

Jai nodded. "It's good."

Nandu let out a laugh. "Good? He is having the time of his life working with celebrities, especially with Karina Sehgal."

Seema smiled when she saw Jai turn red in the face. "Glad to hear you are having fun. Make sure you have practice sessions with Riya's fiancé as well."

"Yes, Seema. I am working with both families."

"Jai, I want a sequence for Riya to have a dance with a family member after the group performances. Can you work on that?"

"Who is she dancing with? Another celebrity?" Nandu rubbed her hands together.

Seema shook her head. "Not sure yet, maybe Riya's brother or another family member."

The entire room fell silent like people could not believe their ears. It had been a week since the engagement party, and the team is still dreading to talk about Mr. Brozilla.

"Guys, Riya would love to dance with her brother. It doesn't hurt to try."

"Seema, I can't deal with him." Jai was the first to speak up.

"What? Why?" Seema faked ignorance as she could not let her team be intimidated by a demanding client.

Jai snorted. "After the scene he created at the engagement party, I am staying out of the line of fire."

"He had a valid point about our teammates potentially making their guest uncomfortable." Seema maintained a calm tone.

Nandu jumped in. "Really? She is an actress. How could she be uncomfortable with fans looking at her."

"Guys..." she said and paused, making eye contact with every one of her leads who handled different areas of the event and added, "... he is a client and has every right to tell us what they like and don't like. It's our job to take their input and implement the required changes within reason. The students from the cooking school were not being inappropriate but unprofessional. We need to address that as we have not managed an event where we have had celebrities before."

"Okay, I will have a choreography ready for Riya to dance with a family member but not sure if I can teach him separately." Jai sounded unsure.

"We will figure it out. Maybe we get her dad or one of her close cousins to dance with her," Seema assured.

Jai thought for a moment. "What if we don't get enough practice time or Brozilla decides to back out?"

Seema thought for a moment. "It will be a separate performance. Maybe we pair Riya with her dad or her favorite male cousin, and cut her brother's dance."

"That's a wonderful and safe idea." Nandu sounded excited.

"Yes." Seema let out a nervous laugh as she was not willing not to try to get Riya's brother to dance.

I am going to work on getting him to agree to dance, but I don't know how yet.

"Now, can we talk about the bride and groom intro event? We have less than a week before the event."

Nandu was the first one to interject. "We need to talk about something else before that."

"What?" Seema was surprised Nandu had not mentioned anything earlier in the day.

"Mr. Rayudu just announced the formation of the Janatha Seva Party, and their official ceremony and first rally are on the same day as Riya's bachelorette party."

Seema shrugged. "What does a political party formation have to do with Riya's party that is five weeks later?"

Nandu pulled up the map of the area on her computer and flipped the screen toward Seema. "This is where the hotel we reserved for the weekend is located, and here is the route the party leaders and followers are going to take for a procession before they gather at this auditorium."

Seema thought for a moment. "Are they closing the traffic for the procession?"

"Most likely. And they could close the area down as early as two in the afternoon."

Seema shook her head. "That will mess up the Friday night party."

"We should change the date for the event."

"No, we cannot. Riya's friends are flying from out of town for the event and most of their travel is already reserved. We cannot separate the party from the other activities planned for the weekend." Seema could tell Nandu was about to have a panic attack.

"Stick to the dates. Look for another venue. Another hotel on the other side of the city," Seema instructed.

"Okay. That's a much better idea." Nandu looked relieved.

"Find a location that allows us to create the same design we showed to Riya." Seema was thinking ahead.

"We need to let her know that we are changing the venue. Should I call her?" Nandu asked.

"I will talk to her. I will set up a meeting with her tomorrow to show her some of Neeraj's costume designs and tell her about the venue change. Have some options ready by the end of the day today. I also want some swatches for fabric from Neeraj for me to introduce the designs to her."

"Are you sure about Neeraj designing the outfits for Riya?" Nandu seemed uncomfortable with the upcoming designer.

"We have no other choice, and if I'm not mistaken, Riya might like his unique designs."

Nandu rolled her eyes. "And if she doesn't, then we keep looking until she finds the dresses she likes."

"Her brother and now she are starting to behave like the typical Bridezilla." Nandu let out a sigh, and Seema knew her friend was under a lot of duress.

"She is not. Stop stressing over nothing. Nandu, get me the reservations for a new venue. Jai, I need the performance choreographed today," Seema teased.

"I have no idea how you can stay so calm." Jai laughed as he got up from his chair and left the room.

Seema looked at her head of catering, Jeevan, and said, "Talk to the students who we hire for the plating. Tell them they are not to step out of the assembling area."

"Sure, Seema. Can we lock in the street food cuisine for the upcoming event?"

"Yes. That's what I presented to her, and she loved the platter selection." Seema smiled.

Jeevan left the room, leaving Nandu and Seema both staring at their laptop screens. A moment of silence later, Nandu cleared her throat, making her look up. "What's up?"

Nandu leaned back and said, "I need to take a break from work for a couple of years."

Seema was taken aback. "You mean two months?"

"No. Two years. I want to join the Janatha Seva Party that is being formed after we are done with Riya's wedding."

"You want to go into politics?" Seema asked.

"No, silly. I want to join as a volunteer and help in any way, so Mr. Rayudu can win the election."

"Seema thought for a moment. "I would love to support your noble thought, but the selfish person in me doesn't want you to go."

"I want to do this, Seema."

"Why?"

Nandu shook her head. "I don't know, but I have this strong need to support the party. It almost feels instinctive just like how you say that you get the feeling that you have a family out there."

Seema nodded. "You know I will support your decision even if it means I won't work with you anymore."

"Oh yes, he is who we need to lead the state and then eventually the country. An educated man who gave up his job as a government official to serve the people."

"I believe in you." Seema hugged her best friend.

"Did you hear back from Mr. Sangha on the new investigation?" Nandu asked as she gathered her computer and files.

"He is still waiting for the funding from the university to pick up this research." Seema let out a sigh, not wanting to feel dejected by the fact that she had been through three different investigators who had not found any clue to her roots.

Seema wanted to know what she was made of and why she had this undying feeling that told her she was not an orphan, although she grew up as one, moving from one orphanage to another every few years.

3

Did Riya finalize her outfit for the wedding and reception? Do we have the décor plan drafted?" Seema asked, looking at her team during their Friday morning meeting.

Nandu shook her head. "She says she is not set on a dress yet."

Seema let out a sigh. "Can we get the designers to give us the details of the outfits, so we can plan for the props and decoration? They can work with Riya on the style."

"That's a negative, Seema. Riya is yet to like a dress that she wants to wear for the reception and other events." Nandu sounded frustrated.

"What about the wedding saree? That should be set because I know Riya's mother had chosen that for her."

"Nope. Riya confirmed she will not be wearing one of those sarees. She wants the designer to make her a custom saree with the traditional silk."

Seema thought for a moment. "Have Neeraj get in touch with Riya. If she has not liked any of the designers' outfits, she is not going to find anything she likes."

"Neeraj is not in the same league as the designers Riya has been working with. Are you sure he can meet her requirements?" Nandu speculated.

"We shall see. She may or may not, but we need to change the strategy."

Nandu nodded, and Seema turned her attention to Jai, her entertainment lead. "How is the performance prep coming along?"

Jai nodded. "It's good."

Nandu let out a laugh. "Good? He is having the time of his life working with celebrities, especially with Karina Sehgal."

Seema smiled when she saw Jai turn red in the face. "Glad to hear you are having fun. Make sure you have practice sessions with Riya's fiancé as well."

"Yes, Seema. I am working with both families."

"Jai, I want a sequence for Riya to have a dance with a family member after the group performances. Can you work on that?"

"Who is she dancing with? Another celebrity?" Nandu rubbed her hands together.

Seema shook her head. "Not sure yet, maybe Riya's brother or another family member."

The entire room fell silent like people could not believe their ears. It had been a week since the engagement party, and the team is still dreading to talk about Mr. Brozilla.

"Guys, Riya would love to dance with her brother. It doesn't hurt to try."

"Seema, I can't deal with him." Jai was the first to speak up.

"What? Why?" Seema faked ignorance as she could not let her team be intimidated by a demanding client.

Jai snorted. "After the scene he created at the engagement party, I am staying out of the line of fire."

"He had a valid point about our teammates potentially making their guest uncomfortable." Seema maintained a calm tone.

Nandu jumped in. "Really? She is an actress. How could she be uncomfortable with fans looking at her."

"Guys..." she said and paused, making eye contact with every one of her leads who handled different areas of the event and added, "... he is a client and has every right to tell us what they like and don't like. It's our job to take their input and implement the required changes within reason. The students from the cooking school were not being inappropriate but unprofessional. We need to address that as we have not managed an event where we have had celebrities before."

"Okay, I will have a choreography ready for Riya to dance with a family member but not sure if I can teach him separately." Jai sounded unsure.

"We will figure it out. Maybe we get her dad or one of her close cousins to dance with her," Seema assured.

Jai thought for a moment. "What if we don't get enough practice time or Brozilla decides to back out?"

Seema thought for a moment. "It will be a separate performance. Maybe we pair Riya with her dad or her favorite male cousin, and cut her brother's dance."

"That's a wonderful and safe idea." Nandu sounded excited.

"Yes." Seema let out a nervous laugh as she was not willing not to try to get Riya's brother to dance.

I am going to work on getting him to agree to dance, but I don't know how yet.

"Now, can we talk about the bride and groom intro event? We have less than a week before the event."

Nandu was the first one to interject. "We need to talk about something else before that."

"What?" Seema was surprised Nandu had not mentioned anything earlier in the day.

"Mr. Rayudu just announced the formation of the Janatha Seva Party, and their official ceremony and first rally are on the same day as Riya's bachelorette party."

Seema shrugged. "What does a political party formation have to do with Riya's party that is five weeks later?"

Nandu pulled up the map of the area on her computer and flipped the screen toward Seema. "This is where the hotel we reserved for the weekend is located, and here is the route the party leaders and followers are going to take for a procession before they gather at this auditorium."

Seema thought for a moment. "Are they closing the traffic for the procession?"

"Most likely. And they could close the area down as early as two in the afternoon."

Seema shook her head. "That will mess up the Friday night party."

"We should change the date for the event."

"No, we cannot. Riya's friends are flying from out of town for the event and most of their travel is already reserved. We cannot separate the party from the other activities planned for the weekend." Seema could tell Nandu was about to have a panic attack.

"Stick to the dates. Look for another venue. Another hotel on the other side of the city," Seema instructed.

"Okay. That's a much better idea." Nandu looked relieved.

"Find a location that allows us to create the same design we showed to Riya." Seema was thinking ahead.

"We need to let her know that we are changing the venue. Should I call her?" Nandu asked.

"I will talk to her. I will set up a meeting with her tomorrow to show her some of Neeraj's costume designs and tell her about the venue change. Have some options ready by the end of the day today. I also want some swatches for fabric from Neeraj for me to introduce the designs to her."

"Are you sure about Neeraj designing the outfits for Riya?" Nandu seemed uncomfortable with the upcoming designer.

"We have no other choice, and if I'm not mistaken, Riya might like his unique designs."

Nandu rolled her eyes. "And if she doesn't, then we keep looking until she finds the dresses she likes."

"Her brother and now she are starting to behave like the typical Bridezilla." Nandu let out a sigh, and Seema knew her friend was under a lot of duress.

"She is not. Stop stressing over nothing. Nandu, get me the reservations for a new venue. Jai, I need the performance choreographed today," Seema teased.

"I have no idea how you can stay so calm." Jai laughed as he got up from his chair and left the room.

Seema looked at her head of catering, Jeevan, and said, "Talk to the students who we hire for the plating. Tell them they are not to step out of the assembling area."

"Sure, Seema. Can we lock in the street food cuisine for the upcoming event?"

"Yes. That's what I presented to her, and she loved the platter selection." Seema smiled.

Jeevan left the room, leaving Nandu and Seema both staring at their laptop screens. A moment of silence later, Nandu cleared her throat, making her look up. "What's up?"

Nandu leaned back and said, "I need to take a break from work for a couple of years."

Seema was taken aback. "You mean two months?"

"No. Two years. I want to join the Janatha Seva Party that is being formed after we are done with Riya's wedding."

"You want to go into politics?" Seema asked.

"No, silly. I want to join as a volunteer and help in any way, so Mr. Rayudu can win the election."

"Seema thought for a moment. "I would love to support your noble thought, but the selfish person in me doesn't want you to go."

"I want to do this, Seema."

"Why?"

Nandu shook her head. "I don't know, but I have this strong need to support the party. It almost feels instinctive just like how you say that you get the feeling that you have a family out there."

Seema nodded. "You know I will support your decision even if it means I won't work with you anymore."

"Oh yes, he is who we need to lead the state and then eventually the country. An educated man who gave up his job as a government official to serve the people."

"I believe in you." Seema hugged her best friend.

"Did you hear back from Mr. Sangha on the new investigation?" Nandu asked as she gathered her computer and files.

"He is still waiting for the funding from the university to pick up this research." Seema let out a sigh, not wanting to feel dejected by the fact that she had been through three different investigators who had not found any clue to her roots.

Seema wanted to know what she was made of and why she had this undying feeling that told her she was not an orphan, although she grew up as one, moving from one orphanage to another every few years.

The next morning, Seema pulled up along the elevated, circular driveway of Riya's parents' home and parked her vehicle to one side at the top of the driveway. She was glad Riya was free to meet with her that morning, and she smiled at the young woman who came to the door. She was led to the home office, where she waited for Riya.

Seema placed her computer, purse, and the tote with the catalog from her upcoming- designer friend on the table and looked around the large space. The home office was a large open area with glass walls on three sides of the room. One wall had a beautiful view of the garden in the front yard of the house, one showed the formal living area through the open door, and the other wall was a central focal point of the house that had natural sunlight streaming from the ceiling and a large tree that added a sense of calm to the perfectly decorated home.

She walked over to the last wall that had built-in wooden shelves in with pictures and mementos arranged nicely on the shelves. She stopped when she saw a picture of a young boy holding an electronic circuit in his hands, and the words on the award read

Raghav Vasudev, Genius – Under 10 Category

Her eyes swept over to the next set of mementos that filled the rest of the shelves and realized Riya's brother was a prodigy. As a businessman, he is extremely successful and yet a caring brother, just not a reasonable client.

"Sorry to keep you waiting."

Seema turned when she heard Riya behind her. "No problem. Thank you for taking the time to meet with me on such short notice."

"Not a problem. What's up?" Riya gestured her to be seated at the set of couches to one side of the study.

"I wanted to discuss a couple of things with you... one about your outfits and the other the venue for the bachelorette weekend."

Riya let out a sigh. "I haven't selected my outfits, and I know you need to know the color palette, but—"

"Riya, I'm not here to rush you but to show you some options."

"I have been to every one of the boutiques in the city, and I know what you are going to say about considering someone from another city or going international, but no. I am going to stick to my theme of choosing everything from my hometown. I love this city too much."

"Are you open to a new designer?" Seema asked as she pulled out the folder with the catalog and the swatches.

"I don't care if the designer is new, I want something I like, and you know it has to be unique."

Seema placed the catalog on the small coffee table in front of the couch where Riya was seated and flipped to the page she had marked as an outfit Riya might like. She pointed at the beautiful traditional saree decked with beautiful handwork and said, "I think this style will suit you well."

Riya's eyes widened. "Wow, that's beautiful, and I could use the saree Mom bought me. Neeraj can make the saree unique by adding the handwork I like."

"Yes, and here are some swatches with the kind of handwork the designer creates. Each design is unique as it is handstitched. He is a good friend of mine, and I will make sure he works on your outfits exclusively until the wedding. And everything he makes for you will not be made for anyone else. He is a upcoming local designer who could use your endorsement."

"This is genius. I love the designs. I can't wait to try them on." Riya let out a squeal of joy. "Thank you, Seema. You are the best."

"I am so happy you like the designs. I can leave the catalog and the swatches for you to look through."

"Oh my God, yes. I am so happy I want to scream."

Seema smiled. "I don't know if you will feel the same way when I tell you about the bachelorette event."

Riya laughed. "Bring it on. I feel on the top of the world now that I see hope for having wedding outfits."

"The venue we chose for the bachelorette weekend, The Royal Hotel, we might have to change the venue due to a political party procession."

"Oh, okay." Riya shrugged.

"Riya, you are the best client. Thank you for being—"

Her voice was lost when the glass door to the office opened loudly, and Riya's brother stepped in wearing a t-shirt and shorts. "There you are, Riya. Hello, Ms. Kumar."

Riya laughed as she took the mug of coffee from her brother. "Who the heck is Ms. Kumar."

"Ms. Seema Kumar, would you like some coffee?"

Seema shook her head as Riya continued to laugh at the way her brother addressed her. "I'm fine. Thank you."

"What's with the early morning meeting?" He sat next to his sister on the couch.

"Seema found me an amazing designer. Look at these outfits."

He looked at the catalog and scrunched his nose. "Nice sarees."

"Raghav, look closely at the handwork on the silk." Riya laughed.

"Sure. It is nice." He seemed uninterested as he sipped his coffee.

Seema looked at Riya and said, "Let me know when you are ready to meet Neeraj to get the outfits planned, and I can set up the time for you."

"I will. It would have to be after the family meet-and-greet. I have too much going on before that."

"That works. And I will send you the details of the new location for the bachelorette party and send out the location change notifications."

"What location change?" His tone was curt at best.

Riya turned to look at her brother. "For the bachelorette weekend."

Her brother looked straight at Seema. "You agreed to discuss all changes with me."

"Raghav, stop it. We just discussed it, and I'm good with it."

"Okay, but why are you changing venues? Didn't you spend weeks choosing the right location for each event? Why do you want to change it now?"

"Oh, it's no big deal." Riya tried to brush it away, but her brother was not ready to let go.

"Yes, it is, especially when you spent so much time choosing them." His eyes bore into Seema's as he asked, "Why the change in location?"

"Sir, the Janatha Seva Party has their rally planned for the same day as the bachelorette party, and the police will be blocking off the roads for the day. It will be hard for the guests to get to the hotel for the weekend."

"How do you know they are blocking the roads?"

"My team checked with the local police station, and the route will be blocked for the rally." Seema maintained a calm tone in spite of the way the man was glaring at her like she was making up stories.

He let out a huffed breath and looked at Riya. "Which hotel did you choose for that weekend?"

"The Royal Hotel."

"Why?"

"What do you mean why? I like the hotel. That's why." Riya laughed.

He shook his head. "Why not the Taj or the Novotel? Why did you choose Royal which is a much smaller hotel compared to the others?"

Riya thought for a moment. "Oh, I know. I chose that hotel for the weekend, so we could take up the entire hotel. I know we are going to be loud, so I didn't want other guests complaining about the noise."

Raghav looked at Seema like she had kicked a puppy. "Figure out a way to keep the party at that hotel."

"Mr. Vasudev, it is too risky. The guests will not be able to make it in time if the roads are blocked."

"If the roads are not blocked? Do you not know for certain?"

Seema shook her head. "We won't know for sure until that day, and we cannot wait."

He looked at Seema for a long time before he pulled out his phone and started searching for something. Riya placed her hand on her brother's shoulder and said, "Raghav, relax. It's okay. Having fun is more important."

But he wasn't listening as he put his phone to his ear like he was calling someone. Who was he calling?

Seema and Riya exchanged looks as they heard the sound of a phone ringing as he switched his phone to speaker and placed it on the coffee table in front of him.

"Who are you calling?" Riya whispered.

"The party office contact number from the internet."

"And why—" Riya's words were lost when the ringing stopped, and someone answered the phone.

"Janatha Seva Party office, how can I help you?" A man's voice came through the phone.

Raghav cleared his voice. "Hello, my name is Raghav, and I would like to join Mr. Rayudu for the rally. Can you please tell me if I can join the procession from The Royal Hotel? The route from the party office to the auditorium takes the route by the hotel."

"Mr. Raghav, the rally starts on the south side of the city and not from the party office. Mr. Rayudu wants to cover the older part of the city."

"That's good to know. Thank you!"

"You are welcome. Hope to see you at the rally. Come by the party office sometime and ask for Sravan. I am leading the campaign, and I could use the help of enthusiasts like you."

"Sure, Sravan. Hope to meet you soon." Raghav ended the call and gave Seema a death stare.

"Ms. Seema Kumar, I already told you that I will not tolerate such an oversight."

"But it is still risky to keep the venue for the event. They can change the route anytime because when we checked yesterday, they were going to start from the party office."

"I don't care. The Royal Hotel is the venue. No changes." He sounded adamant.

"What if the roads are blocked, and no one can get to the hotel?" Seema challenged.

"I will have my chopper make trips to bring the guests to the hotel. I'm sure the hotel has a helipad."

Seema was dumbfounded. The man was arrogantly smart. His determination to keep the venue because his sister chose it was commendable, but the way he was behaving, she wanted to scream at him and tell him to stop being a bully. But instead, she managed to smile and nod in agreement.

"Okay."

"Next time you decide to make a change, please make sure you have all the facts before jumping the gun." He stood up and started walking away, making Seema feel like shit. He stopped at the door and looked at Riya. "I'm cooking today. What do you want for lunch?"

"Surprise me!" Riya laughed.

"Ms. Seema Kumar, you should join us for lunch." His tone was surprisingly casual in spite of chastising her a few moments ago.

"Thank you, but I cannot. I have previous plans." She managed to smile as he left. She turned to look at Riya and said, "I'm really sorry I didn't understand the real reason why you chose The Royal Hotel."

"It's no big deal. Raghav is not a fan of last-minute changes and needs to exhaust all options before we switch."

"He is right about not changing. I should have double-checked. We were pretty positive the rally would start from the party office." Seema felt disheartened.

"Seema, it's fine. I want to see his face when he finds out he needs to use his precious office helicopter for personal use." Riya laughed.

"Let's hope everything goes as planned. I'll get going, then." Seema gathered her items and stood up as Riya's phone started to ring.

"I have to take this call, Seema. Sorry, I can't walk with you."

Seema smiled. "No problem. I'll talk to you later." Seema left the home office and stopped outside the room to text Nandu. She typed the message as she walked and let out a gasp when she felt movement in front of her. She stopped abruptly, her phone slipping off her hands as she walked into what initially seemed like a wall.

She looked up to find Riya's brother catch her phone mid-air and hold it in his hand. "Eyes up, Ms. Seema Kumar."

"Thank you, Mr. Vasudev." She made sure to stress his last name as she took the phone from him.

"You are very welcome, Ms. Seema Kumar."

Wow, he knew how to annoy her.

"Have a good day, Mr. Vasudev. Thank you for helping with the route confirmation for the rally."

"Anytime, Ms. Seema Kumar."

Don't let him get under your skin.

Raghav watched her as she walked away from him. He knew he was going out of his way to give her a taste of her own medicine with the formalities. But she seemed to be holding her ground, and he found that amusing.

"I thought you were making lunch for all of us."

He turned to find his sister walking toward him. "I was, and then I came to give Ms. Seema Kumar a sendoff."

Riya let out a laugh. "Why are you being so weird with her name?"

"And you don't find it weird that she is so formal with me?" he grumbled.

"That's how she is. I cringed when she said Ms. Vasudev, and I had to get very creative to get her to call me Riya." His sister chuckled.

"Yeah, she mentioned. I don't know why she has to be so formal."

"It's okay. She is the best."

Raghav let out a sigh and said, "Listen, Riya, I know you like Seema, but you can't let her push you over with her plans."

Riya narrowed her eyes. "Who are you calling a pushover?"

He shook his head. "You hired her to make your events memorable and not stressful."

"She doesn't stress me out." Riya shrugged.

"What about the engagement party? What was that drama about her not letting you change into another dress of your liking."

Riya took a deep breath. "It was not about the dress, so don't blame Seema."

"What do you mean?"

"It was nothing, Raghav."

"Riya, I'm not asking again." He folded his arms looking at his sister.

Riya rolled her eyes. "I had a classic case of cold feet. I was suddenly overwhelmed and got emotional about being a part of another family and all that stuff, and she was there for me. She made up this dress story, so I could openly be upset."

"Do you not want to get married? Why didn't you tell me? We can call off the wedding."

Riya slapped her palm on her forehead. "This is why I didn't tell you. I was overwhelmed and... don't go imagining anything. I love Deepak, and I want to marry him."

"Riya?"

"That's it. Get back to cooking. I need to go check out a new boutique."

"Fine. You can come help me or join Mom and Dad by the pool."

Riya thought for a moment. "You might need some rescuing in the kitchen, so I'll hang out in the kitchen."

Raghav laughed, following his sister to the kitchen as his thoughts wandered to the woman who insisted on addressing him as Mr. Vasudev. He was surprised that the woman who was so formal cared for her clients' feelings and was protective of his sister. He liked that about her.

5

"Guys, make sure everyone is seated for the show. Absolutely no lights inside other than the spotlights on the stage and no movement during the program," Seema emphasized as she spoke into the microphone. They were at a banquet hall with close family on both Riya and Deepak's side for a 'Get to Know the Bride and Groom' event, a couple of weeks later.

"This sounds like protocol for the opera," one of her technicians teased, making her smile.

"Nandu, do we have all the key family members?"

"Yes, everyone is checked in, and we can start the program once everyone is seated."

A few minutes later, Seema was backstage talking to the performers when Nandu buzzed her. "Seema, Riya's brother is not here."

"What? Did he not check-in? I saw him when he arrived."

"Yes, he checked in, but his seat is empty. I don't see him around." Nandu was starting to panic.

"Nandu, stick to the program. Close the doors and have one of the camera folks to sit in Riya's brother's spot and record the show from that vantage point."

"But what about Brozilla?"

Seema thought for a moment. "Find a screen to block the light from the door. I have a feeling he left the party for a phone call."

"What could be more important than his sister's wedding event?" Nandu grumbled.

"Nandu, it's not our job to judge. Don't forget that her brother employs thousands of people like us, so we, of all people, need to be understanding."

"Whatever. You go look for him. We need to start the program before our youngest performers fall asleep." Nandu laughed.

"Okay, get started as planned." Seema walked away from the back of the stage and smiled at the security as she stepped out. "Please make sure the doors stay closed while the show is going on."

Seema walked along the long hallway of the hotel, where they had planned the meet-and-greet of the to-be bride and groom's family. The show that was about to start was a skit to be performed by a cast selected to match how Riya and her fiancé looked from their childhood to adulthood. She could not believe Riya's brother was going to miss it.

She didn't have his phone number and wished she had a way to reach him. She walked to the main lobby of the hotel looking for him and was relieved to see him standing by the patio doors speaking on the phone.

He looked at her as she approached him while speaking on the phone. She gestured to him to go with her as he continued to speak on the phone. "Get everyone out of the building and shut it down. Make sure everyone is accounted for. I will leave as soon as I am able to."

"Mr. Vasudev, is everything okay?"

He let out a sigh. "Had an accident at the factory."

"Hope everyone is safe." She noticed how upset he looked as he followed her back to the banquet hall where the show was about to start.

"Yes. All the workers were able to get out of the building in time."

"Glad to hear. We should hurry, the show is about to start."

"What show?" he asked, surprised.

"You will need to see for yourself, sir."

"If you say so, ma'am." He chuckled.

She instructed the security team to open the doors and reiterated that they were to keep the doors closed until the show was over. The room turned pitch-black as the doors closed behind them, and she suppressed the gasp that almost escaped her when she bumped into him. "No, sir. You will need to watch from here. You cannot walk through the tables."

"What kind of a show is—" His voice was lost when the music came on, and Riya's voice as a little girl played in the background, and her family cheered recognizing her voice. Then followed Deepak's voice that made the other side of the family join in the cheering.

"You will need to watch from here. I have a videographer sitting in your spot to record your experience," she whispered.

"I can get to my seat."

"No, sir. Do not ruin the show for the other guests." Their eyes clashed in the dark, and she saw how annoyance scorched in them, but he did not say anything.

Seema stood to one side of the stage behind all the tables, aware of the man itching to join his family. She knew he wasn't annoyed about not being in the front close to the stage when she heard his chuckle. "That kid looks just like Riya when she was five. That's an uncanny resemblance."

Seema smiled, feeling pride fill her. The show was her brainchild, and because it was a surprise, she could not share the details with anyone, not even Riya. Her team worked hard to gather pictures of Riya and Deepak at different ages and worked on finding actors who best fit their look and features.

She felt a zap of energy pass through her with every sound of sheer joy that Raghav let out, and her thrill hit the peak when he whistled, cheering for the part when the young Riya said her brother was her hero because he fixed her train set.

"Who planned this program?" he asked from behind, leaning close to her.

"I take it that you like the show, Mr. Vasudev?" She smiled, turning her face sideways.

"It's fantastic. I want an encore, and this time I am going to enjoy the show from my special seat." His breath was hot in her ear.

"But, sir—"

"Make it happen, Ms. Seema Kumar."

She hesitated for a moment. "I would if you stopped addressing me by my full name. Seema is good."

She saw the glint in his eyes, even in the dark, as he smiled. "Consider it done."

Seema pressed on her earpiece. "The guests love it. Let's tee up for a quick encore of the show. Maybe a part of the show if not all of it."

"Thank you, Seema." His words were a whisper, and the way he said her name made her heart warm.

"You are welcome, Mr. Vasudev."

Later that evening, she was in the kitchen area checking on the dessert plating when Nandu's voice came through Seema's headset.

"Seema, there is a somewhat unhappy-looking guest who wants to talk to you." Her heart sank.

Now what?

"On my way." She made it out of the plating area and rushed back to the banquet hall. The event was a success, and based on the social media tags she got for her business, she knew she had a happy client and guests.

She approached Nandu and had barely asked about the guest when she saw Riya's brother and an older gentleman approach them.

"That's who wanted to talk to you," Nandu whispered and slipped away.

"Hello, sir. How can I help?" She smiled.

"Seema, this was a wonderful event, and I would love for you to host my wife's birthday party next month."

Seema could guess why Nandu had said he was unhappy when he spoke to her. "Sir, we would love to manage your event, but unfortunately, I cannot until after Riya's wedding."

"I assure you, my wife's birthday is two weeks before the wedding, so there will be plenty of time. And Riya has no objection for you to organize my party."

Seema pressed her lips together. "I apologize, sir. We only manage one event at a time. We like to stay focused on our clients' needs, which is what has made our team successful."

The older man nodded understandingly, and she was relieved. "I guess I will get in line."

Seema laughed. "Please share your contact details with us, and we will be in touch."

The older man reached into his jacket pocket and handed her his business card. "I am happy to see your business is not as commercialized as the others. While others are looking to take on every event they can get, here you are focusing on one client at a time."

"Thank you so much, sir, for understanding."

The older man bid his goodbye and left her standing with him. *Brozilla.*

She held his gaze as their eyes locked in silence for a long moment. "Nice event. I like what you did tonight. And I am told it was your idea."

"Team effort, Mr. Vasudev."

He let out a sigh. "I can't tell you how much I despise being addressed so formally."

"Sir, it's out of respect."

"Right!! I think I prefer Brozilla." He chuckled, and her heart dropped to her stomach.

How did he know? On shit!

She could feel the blood drain from her face as he stood in front of her, smiling.

Is he not mad?

"What is it going to be, Ms. Seema Kumar? Brozilla or Raghav?"

"Sir, I am very sorry. We don't mean to offend you, but—"

He let out a laugh. "It's funny."

"Sir, I will make sure the team addresses you by your first name as you prefer."

"Now we're talking. Everyone uses my first name, no 'sir' business with me?" He wagged his long index finger.

Sure... Raghav s-sii... I will let the team know." She almost added *sir* after his name by habit and stopped when he raised his eyebrow.

"Thank you!" He started to turn away from her.

"Raghav, one more request. Please consider participating in the Sangeet ceremony performances. It would top all the surprises we have planned for Riya."

He thought for a moment. "Bigger surprise than tonight?"

"Yes. You are the last person she would expect to dance, and I know how much you love your sister. I saw the way your eyes sparkled when you saw her squeal with joy. Please."

He smiled. "Not sure about how much Riya wants to see me dance. I get the feeling you want to see me dance."

She felt a wave of embarrassment sweep over her. "No, sir... I mean Raghav. This is for Riya."

"I'll think about it and let you know."

"Can I have your phone number? I can remind you in case you forget."

He gave her his phone number and said, "Send me a text so I can save your phone number."

"Sure. I will connect with you tomorrow. We can discuss the plan then."

He scoffed. "You're so sure I will dance that you want to discuss the plan?"

"I already have a plan. I just need your confirmation."

He looked around the banquet hall at his sister for a brief moment and saw her take pictures with her fiancé, her smile bringing a glow to her face.

Seema saw him smile as he looked at his sister before turning to look at Seema. "What the heck, let's do it."

"Yes!"

"But under one condition."

"What is that?" Seema was overjoyed.

"Plan it in such a way no one knows, and if I can't pull it off, then you should be able to cancel it."

Seema smiled when she realized she had the exact same thought about his dance. "Deal."

He took her hand she had extended and shook it. "I can't believe I got myself into this."

"Me neither, but this is great. I will be in touch." Seema walked away from him, feeling his eyes on her.

Brozilla isn't that bad, after all.

Seema was in a different state of mind as she walked through the lobby of Vasudev Corporation a few days later. She had the plan laid out for the bride's brother to give Riya the biggest surprise with his grand dance performance.

It was a secret performance that not even her lead, Jai, knew about. Jai was under the impression that he was choreographing a performance for Riya and her cousin, Ravi. Seema's plan was to have Riya perform with her teenage cousin and then have an encore, where Raghav dances in place of the bride's cousin, the second time. She would have to plan a transition that day for the dance so Raghav can close the event with a bang. A smile formed on her face as she rode the elevator to the top floor at the idea of how thrilled her client was going to be.

"Hello, dear." Mrs. Sharma, smiled from behind her desk.

"Good to see you, Mrs. Sharma."

The older woman waved away the formality. "Please call me Kamala."

Seema let out a laugh. "I just got used to calling Raghav by his first name. You'll have to cut me some slack."

"Good, you kids figured that out."

"Yes, we did." She felt the heat creep up her cheek at the memory of Raghav revealing his knowledge of the term

Brozilla.

"He is done with his meeting, just wrapping up some emails. What event are you guys reviewing today?" the older woman asked.

"The bachelorette weekend events." A surprise has to be kept a secret from everyone, including Raghav's trusted assistant, as she was in contact with Riya.

"I am so happy for Riya and Deepak and Raghav—"

"Did someone say my name?" Raghav's voice came from behind, and Seema felt a zap of energy pass through her. It reminded her of the time he stood behind her the evening of the party where he watched the show with her.

"He is all yours, Seema. I am heading home now."

"Good night, Kamala ma'am."

Seema nodded at the elderly woman before turning away from her to walk into his office. She walked past him, barely making eye contact as she suddenly felt nervous about the idea of her teaching him how to dance.

Why does it matter?

She took a deep breath, gathering the strength from her professionalism to teach him to dance. The strange sensations were annoying, and she dismissed them as an appreciation and admiration to what the man was willing to do for his little sister.

"I have no idea what I signed up for." He chuckled, loosening his tie.

"You will be fine. No one, other than the two of us, know about this."

"Really? Not even your team?"

"That is correct, and I would like to keep it that way." Seema held her chin high with pride.

"And who is going to teach me to dance?"

"I can teach you. I have done that in the past."

He nodded, the end of his mouth twisting up. "Multi-talented, are we, Ms. Seema Kumar."

"Mr. Vasudev, like I said before, I prefer Seema." She smiled.

He laughed, shaking his head. "I hear you loud and clear."

"Let's start." She set her phone on his desk and added, "The plan is for you to dance with Karina. Your cousin, Ravi, and Karina are paired and are practicing dancing to this song."

"And you will switch on the day of the Sangeet?"

"Yes." Seema was confident with her plan.

"And you will let Ravi and Karina perform if I decide to pull out." He kept his eyes locked with hers.

"You won't, but yes, it will be as if that was what was planned."

"And no one else knows?" he asked.

"Yes. I will work with you, taking your schedule into consideration."

He let out a sigh as if unable to believe he signed up for this.

"It'll be easy. I will break the steps down for you, and all it takes is to memorize the sequence."

"Sure. Easy-peasy." He chuckled.

"That's right. First, we start with the basic moves. I want you to practice these anytime you have a few minutes."

"Okay."

"I'm serious, you need just these five moves, and the choreography will fall into place."

"And you know this, how?" He raised a curious eyebrow.

"It's part of what I do. My first job in the event management business was to teach the little kids how to dance."

"Did you just call me a kid?" He faked shock.

She bit her lip to stop the smile from widening. "I didn't, but I can tell you are looking for an excuse to get out of this."

He shook his head, smiling, "Okay, I guess I have to do this."

"Yes, and I can coach you over a video chat if we cannot meet in person."

"Wow, there is no escape from you."

"Remember, it's all for Riya." She let out a laugh.

"Why is she so important to you?" He leaned on his heavy desk as he rolled his dress shirt sleeves.

She was puzzled. "I don't understand."

"Why go out of your way to get me to participate. It's not like you get paid extra for making me dance."

She pressed her lips and nodded. "Not everything needs to translate into money."

"So, what's your motivation?"

No client had ever asked her why she did things the way she did, almost with a level of obsession. "I love my job. I like making my clients happy."

"What's in it for you? It's not like you are taking on all the events that come your way. Why go to this length?"

She knew he hit the nail on the head, and she stood in silence as he looked at her, wondering if she should tell him the real reason. Her pragmatic side shut her down. She was not going to open up to a stranger, a client, about how much joy weddings give her, the family bonding she gets to see while organizing a wedding was her way of filling the void she felt deep inside.

"Weddings are fun, and I take my clients' happiness and joy very seriously. Now can we get started?"

"Yes, ma'am." He chuckled.

*****

"Why would someone who works for the Janatha Seva party send us an email?" Nandu seemed unsure.

"Not really sure, but let's see what they have to say. Can you confirm the route of the rally again, just in case they changed it?"

"Using the same number from their website?"

"Yes, Raghav did an internet search on his phone and found the number."

"Raghav? You were quick to make the shift to address him that way," Nandu teased.

Seema rolled her eyes. "I wasn't calling him Brozilla like you all got used to, that's why."

Nandu laughed. "It's nice of him to be cool about the nickname we gave him."

"He is a pretty cool guy." She smiled, thinking of the time she spent teaching him how to dance the previous evening.

"Impressed, are we?" Nandu was not going to let go.

"Here, I found a number, and I think the man who Raghav spoke to is Sravan. You should use this number." Seema showed the number on her phone.

Nandu looked at the number on Seema's screen and the one she had in the message they received from their website, and it was the same number. "I think we can kill two birds with one stone."

"What?" Seema scrunched her nose.

"Looks like it's the same person who is interested in doing business with us. The name is Sravan."

"Okay, we can ask about the rally route at the same time." Seema dialed the number from her desk phone and turned on the speaker. The other end of the line rang for a long time before a man answered it.

"Hi, this is Seema from 'Basket of Gold' events company. I am looking to speak to Sravan."

"Hello, Seema, thank you for calling me."

"Sir, thank you for your interest in our work. How may we assist you?"

"My brother and I would like to plan a surprise anniversary party for our parents. I hear you are good at hosting unique events. We need a party planned in my father's native village and arrangements made for various events."

"What weekend were you thinking, sir?"

"Sravan, please," he said and mentioned a date that was a few months out.

"Sure. We are currently working on a wedding, and we will start laying some groundwork for your event toward the end of the wedding. We will start working on the execution of your event only after we wrap up everything with our current project."

"Okay. We want this to be special but extremely private. No media or anyone not on the guestlist should know any of the details."

"Understood."

"Thank you. Can we set up a time to discuss your thoughts on what you want for your parents' anniversary?"

The man went silent for a moment. "We don't have anything specific, but I would like to meet when my older brother is also available. He is away on business and will be back in a few weeks. Can you meet at our party office in a few weeks?"

"Sounds good, sir... I mean Sravan. A few weeks will the seventeenth of next month, and are you available at ten in the morning?" Seema believed in putting a stake in the ground, especially with a new client.

"Yes, I am."

"Good. The number I am calling from is the best number to reach me," Seema said and added, "I also have a question about the rally route on the formation day. Is it still from the old city and not from the head office?"

"Yes, and it will stay that way. Why do you ask?"

"My client's pre-wedding event is planned at The Royal Hotel, and I am asking to make sure the roads won't be blocked."

"Okay. They won't be."

"Thank you, have a good day." Seema ended the call with a wide grin, and Nandu let out a squeal of joy.

"I guess this is the same man Brozilla talked to?" Nandu giggled.

"Yes, same person. *Raghav* spoke to Sravan Rayudu. He is also listed as the campaign manager."

"Yeah, yeah... Raghav, not Brozilla." Nandu typed something on her computer and added, "Guess what? The guy you spoke to is Mr. Rayudu's younger son. Twenty-four years old, recently returned from studying and working abroad, and instead of joining his older brother in business, he joined his father to run his political campaign."

"Such a kid by age, but he sounded mature."

"Don't call him a kid. He is only three years younger than us." Nandu laughed.

"Okay, now I need to sort out the investigation."

"Seriously, Seema. You are going to start another one like you didn't spend enough money on the other three the last few years?"

Seema shook her head. "This is different. Our old client, Mr. Sangha, is going to take up my investigation as part of his research and is waiting for the approval from his department head."

"Yeah, but you will still need to hire an investigator to reach out to whoever they find as a DNA match."

"I have to keep trying."

"But why? Why does it matter now? You don't need a family. You are doing really well for yourself."

"More than a family, I want to know what I am made of... my roots."

Nandu let out a sigh. "Listen, what if you find a family and realize they got rid of you. I don't know... maybe an unwanted pregnancy."

Seema shrugged as a lump formed in her throat. "It doesn't matter. I want to know where I belong. My culture, language... I know nothing."

"It's no use. I have a family, I know my roots, but what's the point? My parents are divorced, and they still fight over me like I am an object and not their child."

"You have no idea." Seema shook her head.

"I still think you should let it go. I have seen you go through so much heartbreak when the other investigations were unsuccessful."

"I know, but I am hopeful about this research."

"Bad idea."

"Why?" Seema scrunched her nose.

Nandu took a deep breath and said, "I love you, and don't get me wrong when you hear this."

"What?"

"What if... you were an unwanted child, like by, I mean... like a prostitute who got pregnant or even an illegitimate one."

Seema shrugged. "Whatever it is, I just want to know."

"I just don't want you to be hurt."

"I know. Thank you. Now get working on the ideas for the Rayudu event. Just ideas and Riya's events are still our top priority."

"Yes, ma'am." Nandu laughed, and Seema smiled as her thoughts wandered over to the man she had been thinking a lot about lately.

Why was she wondering what he was doing?

Because she was hoping he was practicing the dance moves.

7

"I'm not happy with the menu for the outdoor camping. This food can get cold very fast. Switch to items that can be made quickly when ordered." Seema looked at one of the short-listed food vendors for the event coming up in a few weeks.

"Okay, I will update the plan and send it to you."

"By the end of tomorrow, please. I have another vendor who has a plan my team likes, but I want to see yours as I think you can do better."

The woman who owned the catering service smiled. "Thank you for the opportunity. I will send you an updated menu soon."

"Thank you." Seema looked at her phone after the woman left and had noticed that Riya had messaged and called her.

She called Riya back and said when her client answered, "Sorry, Riya, I was in a meeting."

"No problem. Are you free to meet me now?"

"Like now? Where are you?"

Riya let out a laugh. "I'm not taking no for an answer. The car is on the way to pick you up. Meet me at Neeraj's boutique. I need your help. I'll text you when the car arrives."

Before Riya could ask if anything was wrong, she ended the call. Seema messaged Nandu about her leaving the office to meet Riya and waited for her ride to arrive. She was in the middle of reviewing the props option for the reception that was six weeks away when her phone buzzed a notification.

She picked up her purse and her computer and headed downstairs to the lobby. As she stepped out of the elevator, she saw a car waiting outside the main doors of the building. She took out her phone to ask Riya the make and color of the car, and just then, another message showed up.

Her lips curved up inadvertently when she saw the message.

Raghav: *Ms. Seema Kumar. Don't look at your ride suspiciously.*

She bit her lip as she stepped out of the lobby and walked toward the car. She smiled at Raghav as he looked at her, his eyes hidden behind dark aviator sunglasses.

"Hello, thank you for being my ride."

"Sure."

Seema noticed a few moments later that Raghav was not in his usual suit and tie attire, and he had on what looked like a uniform—an olive-colored shirt with matching trousers with a logo stitched on the pocket. She noticed how his sleeves were rolled up, and she swore she saw grease stains on his arm.

"What's with the *Top Gun* Tom Cruise look?" The words rolled off her lips before she could contain her curiosity.

He chuckled. "I had a factory visit today."

"Is everything okay from the fire accident?" she asked, remembering the phone conversation he was on the day of the program.

"You remember?"

She nodded, smiling in response to the surprise in his tone. "How is your dance practice coming along?"

He let out a laugh. "Riya almost caught me practicing one of the steps."

"I doubt if she would ever expect you to dance. Her exact words were, *don't even bother asking my brother to dance, he won't.*"

"She was right about that. I don't know how I ended up agreeing."

"Because you want to surprise your sister."

"Right."

"Does Mrs. Sharma know you are practicing?"

"Was she supposed to?"

Seema shook her head. "It's best if she doesn't."

"Especially since Kamala ma'am and my mom are best friends. They don't keep secrets."

"Oh, Mrs. Sharma is your mom's friend and your teacher?"

"Yes."

"It is very nice of her to work with you. It's important to have someone you can trust in that role."

"Absolutely."

"So, do you know why I am needed at Neeraj's boutique?"

He shrugged as he kept his eyes on the road. "I have no idea who this Neeraj is, and I needed to get away from there, so I offered to be your ride."

"Oh, that's very nice of you."

"What? Saving myself from the shopping drama?" He chuckled.

Seema smiled. "For being my ride. What was Riya's response to the outfits."

"I have no idea. She has had my parents hostage since this morning, and I am not sure how long we would be at the boutique."

"Don't make it sound so bad."

"You have no idea. There were racks of clothes she was supposed to try on and rolls of fabric all in the middle of the boutique and no other customers."

"Riya gets exclusive access. Neeraj will work with her until she finds the outfits she likes."

"Did you know Neeraj from before?"

She nodded. "We used to work for the same wedding planner years ago."

"Nice. And I have someone who is looking for an event organizer."

"Thank you for your consideration. I do have something right after Riya's wedding but can take up a project after."

"Just when you start getting all the top projects in the city, why are you still taking up one at a time?"

"Nandu and I will be working on another weekend event. We are looking to expand our teams to take on more after that."

"What is the reason you support only one event at a time?"

"Depends on the type of event. If both Nandu and I need to work on the event, then we don't take on any other event so we can stay focused."

"I take it this is a top client."

"Yes, a political party event." She tried to make it sound generic. She didn't want to give out any more details about the anniversary party she would be arranging for the Rayudu couple.

"Interesting. You into politics?"

"No, just want to support a new leader who is trying to do the right thing."

"Time will tell if a party head will stay a leader or turn into a politician." Raghav kept his eyes on the road, and she was glad the topic shifted away from the private event she was going to work on.

"I will give my best to every event, and thank you for referring my company to your contact."

"You are welcome, but I'm sorry for losing my cool at the engagement party." He kept his eyes on the road, and Seema turned to look at him.

"We already talked about that. There is no need to apologize."

He smiled, his eyes still away from her. "Riya told me everything about the *dress* situation."

She nodded, smiling. "I see."

A silence fell between them, and she didn't like it. She was starting to enjoy talking to him, but she knew it was best to keep communication on an as-needed basis.

"When do we practice next?" he asked.

"Whenever you are free."

"I am going out of town next week and would like to get as much practice in this week. Do you work over the weekends?"

"Absolutely."

"Can we meet on Friday evening and Saturday morning?"

"Sure. Will I have access to your office building?" She started punching in the reminder on her phone.

"No. You can come by my place."

"Seriously? Don't you have a better place for practice?" She tried hard not to roll her eyes, considering he lives in the same house as his parents and sister.

"Why? What's wrong with my place?" He snorted.

"Your dance wouldn't be the best-kept secret, then. How can you keep it from Riya and everyone else?"

His brows furrowed. "Why would Riya be at my place. She would be at my parents' house."

Seema was confused. She was under the impression the entire family lived in the beautiful house she had been to a couple of times. "Are you talking about a different place?"

He chuckled. "I don't live with my parents. I moved in, so I can keep the calm in the house and save my dad from the two panicky women in the house while we prep for the wedding."

Seema smiled, rather embarrassed with her assumption and arguing about it. "That is sweet of you."

"So, can I have two practice sessions before I leave on Sunday?"

"Sure. If I can have a few hours on Saturday morning, I can get the choreography routine also practiced for you."

"Sounds good. I'll take care of the food for us." He smiled, turning to look at her for a brief moment.

"I can't wait to see the surprise and delight in Riya's eyes."

Raghav pulled the car off the street and into the boutique's driveway and smiled as he watched his sister through the glass windows. "Look at the delight in her eyes already."

Seema let out a laugh. "I think she found her wedding outfit."

She pushed open the car door and walked into the modest yet beautiful boutique. "Riya, that color looks beautiful on you."

Riya looked up from holding the skirt and let out a squeal of joy. "Seema, I love you so much for bringing Neeraj into my life."

Neeraj chuckled as he stood up and hugged Seema. "How have you been, sis?"

Riya's eyes widened. "Seema is your sister?"

Neeraj winked. "God-given sister."

"That is so sweet. Neeraj, I want you to design all my outfits. I want you to design for my mom, dad, and Raghav, too."

Seema was glad her recommendation worked out. "Let's have Neeraj take care of your outfit first."

"I don't see Mr. and Mrs. Vasudev around." Seema looked around the empty boutique.

"They snuck out when I was trying on a dress. I'm sure Raghav had something to do with that." She sneered at her brother.

Raghav rolled his eyes. "I'm sure Neeraj is looking to catch a break from you."

"Absolutely not. I will be here as long as Riya has the energy to try on the outfits."

"Great," Riya said, smiling, and added, "Raghav, why don't you order food and drinks for us?"

"I love you so much right now, Riya," Raghav mocked his sister, knowing she was going to hold him hostage at the boutique while she chose her outfits.

Seema smiled and pointed to two plush chairs to one side of the boutique. "Those look comfortable."

"Good idea." Raghav chuckled as he followed her to settle down for an unknown amount of time while the bride-to-be tried on outfit after outfit.

8

"Where are you going?" Nandu asked, sounding suspicious.

Seema picked up her tote with an extra pair of clothes to change into for the dance practice with Raghav that evening and said, "I'm heading to a meeting and then to the gym."

"What meeting? It's Friday night, and we were all supposed to go out for drinks and play poker at Jai's house." Nandu raised a curious eyebrow.

"I am meeting a caterer who seems to have a good platter option. I don't want to miss out on a good option." She felt guilty about lying to her best friend.

Nandu smacked her forehead with her palm. "Lord... and here I was secretly hoping that you were meeting someone."

"Nice." Seema let out a laugh.

"You know organizing weddings is cool, but you need to get your own life. You need to either go on dates or start dating people we meet in our work."

"Not happening." Seema shook her head.

"Then, you need an online profile, so you can start seeing someone. You haven't had a relationship since that prick ruined it all," Nandu grumbled.

Seema rolled her eyes. "It's not because of him that I don't meet other people, it's because of work."

"Then prove me wrong that your ex is not the reason you don't date anymore."

Seema laughed. "I will after Riya's wedding."

"I don't believe you. Then, you'll say after my wedding." Nandu laughed.

"Are you getting married? Who is the lucky guy?" Seema winked.

"I know you will find another excuse and—"

"Nandu, I'm serious. I will create an online matrimonial profile right after Riya's wedding."

"Promise?"

"Yes. I have to go. You guys have fun." Seema left her office and headed to the parking lot.

Seema was excited about the surprise Raghav was about to give his sister. The best gift in she could think of. She followed the instructions to Raghav's place and realized he lived pretty close to his office and was in an upscale apartment complex.

Raghav's parents' mansion was one of the most beautiful homes she had ever been to, and if it were up to her, she would live in that house to be close to the parents and not live on his own as Raghav did. But she knew people enjoyed their freedom. Not everyone obsessed over living with their parents, and she knew it would end up being a fantasy that would never become a reality for her.

It was almost seven by the time she approached the private elevator that took her directly to Raghav's apartment and punched in the code. She had stopped at home on her way to change out of her work clothes. Although not professional attire, she knew it would be easier to practice dancing with some comfortable athletic clothes instead of the pencil skirt and silk blouse she had on that day.

She waited as the elevator rode up to the penthouse and keyed in another passcode to open the doors. The heavy metallic doors opened up to a partially covered outdoor space that had a beautiful view of the city on one side and a sanctuary of plants on the other side.

She could immediately see Riya's touch as a home designer in every aspect of the outdoor space, and the area was just stunning.

She walked to the large double doors, and even before she could ring the bell, the doors opened, and Raghav stood at the door wearing a t-shirt that fit him snugly and a pair of linen lounge pants. "Hi, Seema. C'mon in."

"Thanks. You have a beautiful home." She scanned the beautiful living area. "I see a lot of Riya's touch outside but not so much on the inside."

"Long story, I'll have to tell you sometime." He chuckled.

She nodded and looked toward the entrance. "I think the outdoor space is a good place to practice."

He shrugged. "Whatever you prefer."

"Thanks. I'll wait outside for you."

"What would you like to drink?" Raghav asked as she stepped out onto the covered section of the open area surrounded by plants.

"I'm good. I have my water bottle."

"Are you sure you want to be out here?" he asked, stepping on to the outside space.

"Absolutely. It's so beautiful here, and you will be getting a good workout from the dance, so you might as well get some fresh air."

"I could use a workout. I haven't made it to the gym this week."

"Let's begin. Do you remember the basic steps I taught you when we met at your office?"

"I think so." He shrugged.

"Okay, let's see them." She turned on the upbeat music that was the background for Raghav's performance.

Almost an hour later and multiple repeats of the same step, Seema was unhappy about how Raghav was performing one step.

"It's one step, and people will barely notice. Let's move on," Raghav asked, out of breath.

"No. You are dancing with Riya, and she can very easily make you look bad." She kept her eyes on her phone as she watched the video recording of him doing the step.

"Can we take a break?" he asked.

"Raghav, I know what is happening. Let me show you."

"What will you show me?" Raghav smiled.

Seema went to stand behind him and placed one palm on his shoulder and lifted her toe to touch the back of his knee. "Feel my palm and my toe. You need to sync the shoulder movement and the knee bend for the bounce. Now move, and I will push to show you how far you should go."

He let out a laugh. "You are very hands-on."

Seema pushed on his shoulder and edged too much into the back of his knee, making him step away from her, laughing. "If you think I'm hands-on, you should have worked with Jai. That guy will even show you how far you need to swing your arm and the angle at your elbow."

Their eyes locked as something sizzled in the air between them. He looked away when the elevator dinged and said, "Oh no, Riya is on her way here."

"Oh, no, she can't know." Seema grabbed her phone and water bottle and ran indoors.

"Go in. There is a guest bedroom to your left as soon as you enter."

She stepped in behind the doors when she heard the elevator doors open. "Raghav. You knew I was coming. Did Mom call?"

"What a surprise?" Raghav said, and Seema realized the brother and sister were walking in, so she ran toward the guest bedroom and stood behind the door.

"So much for a secret location to practice," she whispered as her heart beat loudly in her ears.

"Mom sent you a special dish. She suspects you are meeting someone tonight at your place." Riya's words made Seema roll her eyes.

"What made her think that?" Seema followed the conversation between the brother and sister with her ear to the door. She needed to know if Riya was going to come wandering into the room she was in.

"I don't know. She was very hopeful about you meeting someone tonight and maybe get married." Riya laughed.

"Tell Mom I'm happy being single."

"You tell her that when you see her." Riya's voice came from the kitchen, and it sounded like she was moving around the space.

"Okay, I have to go shower. Thanks for bringing me food."

Riya let out a laugh. "Are you trying to get rid of me?"

"No. You can hang out here, but I need to go out."

"Really? So, you are seeing someone tonight?" Riya asked, sounding excited.

"Riya, I have to go. You can hang out if you like, but I am going out for dinner." He was being pushy, but his little sister was getting adamant by the minute.

"Okay, I'll go. But are you meeting someone tonight? And you told Mom and not me. I'm hurt."

Seema bit her lip to stop herself from laughing when she imagined Raghav's face trying so hard to lie to his sister. She found it adorable that he was keeping the secret when it would have been so easy to tell his sister about the dance practice.

"I didn't tell Mom anything. Just because I told her I want to be at my place to get some work done, she just made up things."

"I don't care what Mom thinks. You tell me if you are meeting someone tonight, if not, I'm staying. I'll ask Deepak to come join us."

Seema smiled when she heard Raghav let out a growl. "Fine, I'll tell you but promise you won't tell anyone else." Seema stuck her ear to the door, wondering if he was going to tell her the truth.

"Okay, I won't. I promise."

"I have plans for tonight and tomorrow morning as well. And I am telling you this, so you don't barge in tomorrow morning with another special dish."

Riya let out a squeal of joy, making Seema wonder what was so exciting. "So, you are busy tonight and tomorrow morning. You are having a sleepover, huh?"

Seema felt the heat creep up her cheek as she laughed silently.

"Riya, you had too much fun already. Now go." His tone was suddenly firm.

"Okay, but please if she is the one, let me know so I can ask Seema to block her calendar," Riya said, and Seema bit her lip, pressing her hands into her stomach as she laughed silently.

The interaction between the brother and sister was endearing and funny at the same time.

"No. You will not block anyone's calendar. I am planning to elope." Raghav laughed.

"Raghav, you are literally kicking me out of your house."

"I told you, I'm going to be late."

"Fine, I'll go. But when can I share the secret with everyone?" she asked, and her voice was distant as if she was outside the house already.

Raghav chuckled. "Let's just say everyone will know on the day of the Sangeet."

"Will you bring your date to the party?" Riya asked.

"Bye, Riya."

"You are such a spoiled sport."

"Drive carefully," he said.

"Fine, I'll call you tomorrow."

Seema heard the double doors close, but she waited for a few moments just to be sure. She opened the door when she heard a knock.

"That was close." She smiled.

"Let's practice inside. She might show up again for the sake of it." Raghav laughed, and Seema could not help but join the laughter.

"I only wish I could see your expression while you made up all the excuses to get her to leave."

"She made up most of it." He turned on the music system and added, "You can connect your phone to the speakers, so I get the full effect of the music."

"Look at you, all pumped up for the dance," Seema cheered.

"Now that I made a mention of her finding out on Sangeet, I need to get this right."

"That's the spirit." She laughed as she turned the music on high.

A few hours later, she sat across from him at his dining table, licking her spoon clean of the dessert his mother had sent with Riya. "This is by far the best dessert I have eaten ever."

Raghav smiled. "I'll be sure to tell her that."

Seema shook her head. "Hold off until the Sangeet, and I will tell her myself."

"Sure. You can tell her."

"Raghav, thank you so much for dinner. I can barely move now, let alone drive back home." She wanted to fall asleep on the dining table.

"Feel free to stay the night, especially since we are supposed to meet early tomorrow morning."

The idea of snuggling into bed, any bed, was very tempting, but she wanted to get back home. "Thank you for the offer. I'll get going."

Her phone started to ring as she was about to get up. Nandu was calling. "Seema, are you home yet?"

"No, I'm not. Why? What's happening?"

"What do you mean what's happening? There is a major grid failure, and the entire city is in the dark."

"Oh," she looked up at Raghav who was looking at her puzzled. "I didn't realize there was a power outage. I'll be heading home soon."

Nandu let out a sigh of relief. "Just wanted you to know that I am staying back at Jai's place. The traffic is a mess with the signals out. I will see you in the morning."

"Okay, I'll mostly see you later in the day, then. I'll be leaving early for a meeting."

"Fine. But be careful when you get home. Lock the doors well."

"Yes, I will." Seema ended the call and looked at Raghav. "A grid failure, and you are not impacted?"

He smiled. "Solar power reserve, and the building has a generator if needed."

"Good. I was wondering how far I would make it down the stairs. I'll get going, then. That was some awesome food, and we can burn off the calories tomorrow morning."

"Sounds good."

"I will see you tomorrow at seven thirty?"

"Sure. I will have my security follow you to your place."

Seema shook her head. "That is not necessary."

He smiled. "That was merely for your information."

"Sure, thank you!" Seema stepped into the elevator with a weird feeling settling in. She was not used to people taking care of her, especially not a client. But it felt nice.

How in the world did she end up talking to him for hours? How is it that her mind did not go haywire at the thought of spending hours at someone else's house? It is not something she had ever done. Even if she had joined Nandu at Jai's house, she would have insisted on going back home sooner rather than later, and yet she had spent an entire evening at someone's house, and it was fun.

Maybe because she was having fun dancing. It had been so long since she had done so.

9

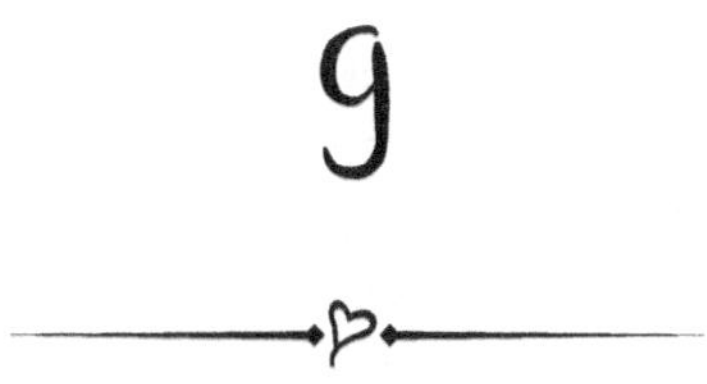

Seema woke up to the alarm on her phone, and it took her a moment to remember why the house was so quiet and everything from the night before. She felt important with professional security following her home to ensure her safety, and that brought a smile to her face. She pulled the sheets around her, enjoying the feel of warmth on that chilly morning.

She could not remember the last time she sat down and ate a meal while having a conversation with someone. Not even with Nandu. And she spent hours talking about everything under the sun and moon with Raghav without getting into personal stuff other than about his sister.

Maybe it was time to get over the need to hunt for a family, start her own family, and expand it with her good friends. If she found the right partner, she could build a family of her own. She closed her eyes and thought about ways to slow down and not think about work all the time. She could not deny the fact that she enjoyed teaching someone how to dance. It helped her take her mind off of the list of things that needed to be done. She made a mental note to start joining her team for happy hour and other social events.

She lay in bed suddenly wide awake, excited about teaching Raghav how to dance. Maybe she could leave early and explore the garden outside his place and maybe even catch a sunrise over the hills, something she had not done in ages. She got out of bed and pulled her messy hair into a ponytail. She showered and grabbed her bag and phone and was out the door in under twenty minutes.

It was still dark outside as she drove toward his house and arrived almost forty-five minutes sooner than planned. It was early spring and still a bit chilly outside, but she couldn't wait to catch her first sight of the beautiful garden in the morning light. She bypassed the lobby check-in since she had the code to the private elevator. She was so lost in the excitement to hang out in the sanctuary that morning by herself, she had initially missed hearing the low beeping sound in the background.

"Shit," she murmured when she realized the beeping had to be a security alarm that would go off, waking up the neighborhood if she didn't turn it off immediately.

People had alarm systems for the outside?

She looked around frantically for the control panel as the beeping got louder by the second. When she saw the screen on the alarm panel counting down from fifteen, she knew there was no way she could turn the alarm off.

She pulled out her phone and called Raghav only to get his voicemail. She looked around for an on-call button, so she could reach the security team, or should she just get back into the elevator and run back home? Maybe she should just wait for the alarm to go off?

"No." She dialed his number again, and this time as the phone rang in her ear, the alarm was turned off.

"Did I oversleep?" His voice was groggy from sleep.

"No. I got here early, and the alarm went off."

He chuckled. "I should have told you last night about the alarm. It's usually on until eight. Would you like some coffee?"

She felt embarrassed for waking him up. "No. Please go back to sleep. We don't start for another forty-five minutes."

"It's all right. I'll see you in a bit."

"Okay." She ended the call and smacked her forehead with her palm. "Such an Einstein you are, Seema."

She looked at the alarm panel to make sure it was turned off before she walked around the open space. Relieved that nothing went off this time, she took in the chilly morning air and was blown away by the beauty of the space.

"Wow," she said, looking at the sun coming up over the hills at a distance. She walked through the covered porch lined with the plants toward the railing. She could not believe the view from the terrace and was lost in thought until she sensed movement behind her.

"Good morning," his voice was soft."

She turned to look at him, still feeling embarrassed about waking him up so early. "I'm so sorry."

"Seema, cut it out. It's no big deal. Here is your coffee." He placed the mug of steaming hot liquid in her hand and sat on one of the patio chairs.

She sat across from him and noticed him cringe as he sat down. "Are you okay?"

He nodded, taking a sip of his coffee. "I think I pulled a muscle with all the dancing."

"Oh, where?" She leaned forward to look at his leg.

"I'm fine. I just need to stretch it out."

"I'll help you warm up and stretch before we start the practice today."

"Sure. Sounds like I have no escape now." He grinned.

"This is a beautiful view." She took a sip of her coffee.

"I love it, too, just don't spend enough time here."

She looked around the space they were in and asked, "You let Riya design only the outdoors, how come?"

He snorted. "I didn't like what she wanted to do on the inside."

She smiled. "What happened to the loving brother?"

He shook his head. "Loving but not blind."

"Was she upset?"

He chuckled. "Oh, she didn't talk to me for a week, and then I had to make her one of her favorite dishes and offer a peace treaty. So, we settled for the outdoors."

"She did a wonderful job. She is super talented."

"That she is." He smiled, pride filling his eyes. "And for the record, I did let her decorate a wall inside the house."

"That's sweet. Can I see the wall? I might use it as an idea for one of the backgrounds for the upcoming events."

He looked at her for a long moment. "Do you ever stop working?"

She felt the heat creep to her cheeks. "I do. I did last night when I was enjoying the amazing food."

"I doubt it. I'm sure you were figuring out how you could get the flavors incorporated in the food for the events."

She let out a gasp and almost choked on the sip of coffee. "I'd be lying if I said that thought didn't cross my mind."

"I knew it." He let out a victorious laugh.

"It's how we keep our events fresh and customized for the client. Is there any way I can get the recipe for Riya's favorite foods? I will work on getting them added to the menu, especially for the camping night food."

He thought for a moment. "I'll think about it and text you the ones I've made for her."

"Amazing. I should have gotten more time with you sooner. I can see how we can make things to Riya's liking."

"Are you like this with all your clients or just with Riya?"

"Why do you ask?"

"Just curious."

She thought for a moment. "I haven't had a client like Riya. She was the first one who challenged me to make everything about her wedding unique, and she gave us a ton of freedom."

"I like what you have done so far."

"Thank you. That means a lot to my team and me."

He nodded. "What can I make you for breakfast?"

She shook her head. "Oh, I don't eat breakfast. Coffee is good."

"You can't be my guest and not have my breakfast. What do you prefer? Eggs or pancakes?"

"You're serious?"

"Do you see me laughing?" he mocked.

"What do you prefer?"

He looked at her for a long moment. "I prefer eggs, but I can tell you like pancakes. Let's get some practice in, and we can eat after."

Is he reading my mind?

Almost two hours later, Raghav stepped away to take a phone call mid-practice. She looked around the large living area that they had practiced in and noticed a beautiful wall with pictures that she had missed earlier.

The wall was painted jet black, and a blue reclaimed wood table fit perfectly along the width of the wall, highlighting the dark background. In the middle of the wall was a large picture of a family. She stepped closer, and she recognized the elderly couple to be Riya's paternal grandparents and then her parents and her cousins, all of them standing in front of what looked like an old-fashioned mansion. She let out a squeal of joy when she realized it was a family portrait with multiple generations.

"I see you found the wall." Raghav chuckled as he walked down the hallway.

"These pictures, they are beautiful." She could not understand why she was getting emotional looking at the various family photos.

"Yeah, that's my family, and I'm sure you've met and dealt with almost everyone."

"Yes. Where was this picture taken?" Moisture gathered in her eyes, and she blinked it away frantically.

"That's in my grandfather's village. We have a family reunion at the house every year, and it is so much fun."

"Beautiful pictures." Her voice was weak with emotion.

"What do you think of the wall?"

"It's stunning. The table, the pictures... amazing."

"You think I should let Riya loose on the rest of the house?" He laughed.

"I would." She smiled, keeping her eyes on the pictures as she let the moisture in her eyes disappear.

"Ready to rock 'n' roll?"

"Yes." She looked away from the pictures, trying hard to swallow the lump that formed in her throat. Just when she thought about making peace with the investigation, something like this pops up, and the undying need to find her roots aggravates her.

She shook away the sorrow that threatened to encompass her and looked at Raghav. "We need a couple more rounds of practice. I see you are still limping. Let me fix that first."

"What do you mean fix that?" He shook his head.

"Let's do a new dance step, and your so-called muscle pull will disappear magically." She managed to smile while pushing away her thoughts of melancholy.

"I believe you," he said, his eyes dancing at her.

10

"What a party! And we are just now getting started," Nandu cheered, and Seema smiled in response to the excitement in her voice over her headset.

"This is an awesome hotel for such a party. I'm so glad we didn't change the venue."

"Why do I not see you on the dance floor?" Nandu giggled.

"You know me. I like watching from the control tower." Seema smiled, scanning her eyes across the security cameras.

"Are you sure you don't want to hang out—"

"I lost you, Nandu." She pressed into the earpiece.

After a lot of static, Nandu's voice came through. "Did you have Brozilla on the list of attendees?"

"Why do you ask? And we don't call him that anymore," Seema warned.

"I know. But it's such a cute name. I can't get over it."

Seema looked through her list and saw that Raghav had declined the event. "He is not supposed to attend."

"Well, Brozilla is in the house, and he is on the prowl." Nandu laughed.

"Nandu, did you have too much to drink?"

Her friend giggled. "Maybe I did, but I am off duty in five minutes. I got morning breakfast duty. So do you, you should go sleep. Leave it to Jai and crew to take care of the party."

"Yes, lock down all the entrances. No one in and out without approval from either you or me."

"Done. Good night. I am going to go catch some sleep."

"Yeah, rest up. We have a busy day tomorrow," Seema said and switched the channel to talk to Jai.

"Jai, you are in charge for the rest of the night. The hotel staff will assist with anything you need and call me if someone needs to go out or come into the hotel."

"You got it, Seema."

"You guys have fun." She smiled as she took off the headphones.

"What about you? No fun for you?" The voice that she was least expecting to hear that night made her smile broadly.

"Hi, Raghav, good to see you. We weren't expecting you." She was surprised to see him in a t-shirt and a pair of shorts. Like he showed up to take a peek and not to be a part of the celebration.

"Sorry to disappoint you." He smirked.

"Not at all. Glad you were able to join. Will you be staying the night?"

He shook his head. "I have to go. I came by to make sure Riya is doing okay."

"She would have loved for you to join the party."

He scoffed. "It's her bachelorette party. I doubt if she wants her big brother around."

"Would you like to grab a drink?" She pointed to the bar.

He shook his head. "I have an early start."

"Do you have time for a round of dance practice?" she asked half-jokingly.

"I thought you'd never ask."

"Very well, then. Time to dance, I guess." She smiled, leading him out of the security room and toward the conference room on that floor.

"Is everything in order for the camping trip tomorrow?"

"Yes, sir."

"Thank you, ma'am," he said, making her smile.

"Will you be joining us tomorrow for the camping event?"

"No. I think you have it all under control." He followed her down the hallway.

She turned when they got close to the conference room. "I wasn't asking you to go to make sure things are in order but to be a part of the event. It'll be fun. A hike, campfire, food, and camping under the stars."

"Sounds like fun."

"We will count you in, then."

"Sure." He shrugged, stepping into the conference room and closing the door behind him.

Seema pulled out her phone and asked, "Have you been practicing?"

"Maybe."

"Let's see how you do."

He shook his head. "I need you to dance along so I know I am following the sequence."

She smiled, kicking off her shoes. "Let's see how well you practiced. Riya has been perfecting the steps with your cousin."

"Really? I'll beat anyone at this dance," he boasted playfully.

"Are you challenging your dance coach to a dance-off?" She laughed.

"Maybe. Is my dance coach too chicken to dance with me?"

Seema narrowed her eyes. "Never."

"Fine. Pick a song, and I will show you my real dancing skills." He let out a growl.

"Really? Then why all this hidden drama for you to dance with your sister?" she teased.

"I'm not into dancing on stage. I dance to the beats in the right ambiance and with a fun dance partner." He winked.

"Let's see if I can be a worthy partner for you."

He scrunched his nose. "You're okay, and I'm awesome, so I can manage."

"Really? Bring it on." She grit her teeth as she picked a fast Bollywood number, one that she used to get a good workout from. And now, something about the way Raghav challenged her, she wanted to show off her dance skills to him.

And she did, each of them taking a bit of the song each to show off their favorite move and eventually got into a copycat mode where Raghav started repeating her moves, driving her nuts.

She made her moves more and more complicated, and she was impressed at how fluidly he moved in the private space but refused to perform in front of a crowd. She laughed when he fumbled at one of the steps and started a victory lap around him, their eyes locked in heated intensity as he stood and bore his eyes into hers.

Halfway through her victory dance, her skirt got tangled between her ankles, and the next thing she knew, she was knocked off her feet. She gasped, knowing she was going to crash the side of her face into one of the chairs or the big table in the conference room.

But her face crashed into his chest, the wind being knocked out of her as his arms circled around her. She gasped a sigh of relief as he held her to him, her feet off the floor. She felt her body shudder from the intensity of the moment.

She realized she had her one arm around him, and the other hand was tightly fisted around the fabric of his t-shirt. She fought for air as he placed her feet back on the ground, and the way his heart beat in his chest matched the rapid beating in hers.

"That was amazing." His breath was hot in her ear as her lungs were filled with the fresh scent of his cologne.

"Sorry, I got carried away." She pulled her arm away from him and let go of his t-shirt.

"It was beautiful. You dance very well."

"Thank you... I... need to go." She turned away from him to hide the crimson that layered her cheeks.

"I'm heading back home. I'll see you tomorrow." His voice was shaky.

"Good night." Without another glance in his direction, she made it straight to her room, her heart pounding in her ears as blood coursed through her veins to meet the thumping in her chest.

What was that? What happened in there? How did I get carried away like that?

*****

"Was he at the party last night?" Riya was excited to hear her brother attended.

Seema nodded as they rode in the bus to the nearby village for the overnight camping trip. "He came to check in on you and left shortly after."

She leaned closer and whispered. "Did he bring a guest with him?"

Seema bit her lip to stop herself from smiling, knowing exactly why Riya was asking. "No. Just him."

"Okay. Just let me know when someone new gets added to the guest list." Riya winked, making Seema smile.

"You got it."

"So, what projects do you have lined up after my wedding?"

"Nothing concrete yet. Why do you ask?"

Riya leaned in closer. "I don't want to jinx it by putting down an advance, but I want you to manage my brother's wedding as well when he decides to marry."

Seema had a tough time keeping a straight face. "Sure, Riya."

"How come you aren't going hiking with us?"

"Nandu and a few other team members are going with you. I will stay back and make sure the tents and the food are ready."

Riya tsked. "I want you to go to have fun. Not to work."

"We have a lot of parties coming up where we can have fun." Seema smiled.

"That's what you say every time. I am going to have a sleepover one of these days, and I want you and Nandu to come."

"Absolutely."

"I had too much fun last night, the DJ was awesome. I was so happy to see all my friends and cousins this weekend. I love this idea of a bachelorette weekend." Riya was cheerful that afternoon.

"So happy to hear you liked the idea. I have some updated ideas for the props we could use for the upcoming events. I will send them to you."

"I love everything you think of, and I'm just so happy, thanks to you." Riya reached out to hug Seema.

"You are a good client, Riya."

"Well, too bad you had to deal with the grouchy Brozilla the first couple of weeks." Riya laughed, making Seema want to hide her face behind the blanket in her hands.

"I'm sorry. It was wrong of us to use a term like that."

"Brozilla, like Bridezilla and Godzilla, it's perfect for Raghav. And I bet you he loves it, too." Riya laughed, and Seema was relieved her client was not offended.

Seema smiled at the thought of Raghav. He was supposed to join them for the camping event, but he had texted Riya at the last minute that he wouldn't be able to attend. The man had been a part of her thoughts lately, and she could not figure out why. Maybe because she had spent time teaching him how to dance, but something was different the previous night when they practiced in the conference room.

The way he instigated her to dance was exceptional, and she had not seen that coming. She admired how he had spent the time to work on his dance moves to be able to dance with his sister.

A few hours later, Seema lay on a blanket under a tree reading a book. The group had left on their hike, and the team on the ground was busy setting up the tents, and the catering team had started prepping for dinner.

She stared at the page and the words, but her mind was drawing a blank. She could not focus on the book, so she decided to put it away and relax.

Her phone buzzed a notification, and she eagerly reached for it. A broad smile appeared on her face when she saw that Raghav was the one who messaged her.

Raghav: *How is the hike?*

Seema: *It's good.*

Raghav: *How do you know? You are not hiking.*

Seema sat up and looked up at the hill, wondering if he had joined them halfway up the hill. She looked at her phone when it buzzed again.

Raghav: *You do look bored out of your mind.*

At that point, she knew he had to be around. She craned her neck to look, and a moment later, he appeared from one of the tents holding two cups of what looked like milk tea.

"You can still catch the group halfway if you drive up the hill and hike down," she called out as he walked toward her.

"No. I'd rather be bored like you." He handed her one of the teacups.

"Thank you. Who said I was bored? I was having the time of my life."

"Right," he said into his teacup.

A silence fell between them as they sipped their drinks, and then she broke it. "You did good last night. Looks like you practiced even when you were away."

"In your own words, I have to surprise and delight Riya." He smiled.

"Oh, by the way, Riya still believes you are going to announce a wedding soon. She asked me to keep my calendar free." She tried hard to keep a straight face.

"Sure. Riya can plan all she wants, but it isn't happening. When I'm ready to get married, I'm going to elope."

"What? No. You can't do that. Your family will be so sad."

He laughed. "That's kind of what I mean. I won't have such a formal ceremony. Just my family."

Seema found the idea to be endearing. "That is so sweet and—"

She looked away at her phone that started ringing. The name of her client, who was a professor at a medical institute, was calling her. It had to be about her investigation. "Sorry, I need to take this."

She answered the call. "Hello, Mr. Sangha, how are you?"

"Seema, I have good news. My department has the approval to fund the DNA research, and your case will be the first one we will be taking up. Congratulations."

"Thank you so much, sir. How can I ever repay you for this?" Tears welled in her eyes.

"Seema, what you did for my family and me during my daughter's wedding, I can never repay you. Please accept this as a form of gratitude."

"Thank you, sir." She ended the call ecstatic about finding another way of reaching her family if she had one.

She looked up through teary eyes to find Raghav looking at her, a slight smile on his face. "Tears of joy, I hope."

She wiped the edge of her eyes and nodded. "Yes. News I have been waiting to hear for months, finally a ray of hope."

Raghav nodded but did not probe. But she felt this undying need to share the news with him. "I finally have a good way to find my family. The people I have only wondered about, I may meet them soon if they are out there."

"That's very good. I take it that you have tried in the past and were unsuccessful."

"Yes, three private investigators and no information," she grumbled.

"When did you lose touch with your family?" he asked, almost apprehensively.

She had never discussed her personal life with any of her clients, not even Riya, but at that moment, she wanted to tell him everything, like she needed to tell him everything about her. "I grew up without anyone, and every day, the need to find family has been growing, and today... I'm so happy."

"Good for you. I hope you get to know more about yourself."

Seema let out a laugh. "Thank you for saying that. I have had to explain to so many of my friends why I poured money into so many different investigators."

"I get it." He nodded. "And being in this business probably adds to the zeal to look for a family."

"Yes. I got into this business for that reason. I wasn't sure if I could ever experience such affection and emotions up close, so I love being in the business of wedding planning."

"Good for you."

She suddenly became aware that she had shared a very personal matter with a client. "I'm sorry, I didn't mean to get into my personal life."

Raghav smiled. "Not at all. For everything you do for my family and especially for Riya, the least I could do is listen to you. Get everything off your chest."

"Thank you. It would be a huge relief when I find out about my roots, and Nandu thinks it's because of this guy who mocked me for not knowing my background, but it is for me."

"I get it. Knowing the fabric we are made of is very important."

She scoffed. "I speak five different languages, and I don't know what my parents used to speak. I don't know what my cultural bindings are, and I can't wait to find out."

He nodded. "How is your current investigation different from the others?"

She smiled, happy there was someone curious about her investigations. "The past ones have been based on the single lead that I grew up in an orphanage in the neighboring state. This one is DNA match based, and one of my clients, who is a research professor at a medical institute, is taking up my case for this research. They will match my DNA with the samples available across all government and private labs as part of the research."

"That's awesome. I hope you find your family soon."

"Me, too. I have good friends, but I want to know who my people are." Her voice weakened suddenly.

As if he noticed the shift in her tone, he lowered his voice and said, "Look around you. Every single one of them are *your* people. You work so hard to bring joy to everyone around you, you will always be surrounded by people who love you."

"Thanks, Raghav, for listening."

"Anytime. Now, if you'll excuse me, I want a fire started before I freeze."

She smiled as she watched him walk away to grab stacks of wood. He looked at her, their eyes locked even from afar, and she felt a fire start within her. She looked away, unable to believe how relieved she felt sharing something she had kept hidden from everyone, and to some extent, even Nandu.

11

"Last fun party before the serious ones in a couple of weeks. I'm getting nervous," Nandu confessed over the walkie-talkie.

"Don't be nervous, Nandu. We got this," Jai said, making Seema smile.

She was blessed to have a wonderful team. W the biggest project of her career, she could not have pulled it off without the team of dozens. "Jai's right. We got this, guys. Who is covering Deepak tonight?"

"I got him." Nandu's voice came through Seema's earpiece.

"I'll keep an eye on Riya." Seema's eyes scanned the club that was decked out for the most talked-about party in town.

"And that leaves me with Brozilla?" Jai laughed.

"Don't call him that. The boss lady doesn't like it." Nandu giggled.

Seema glared at her best friend across the dance floor, making her laugh.

"Really? What do we call him now? Mr. Nice Guy?" Jai teased.

Nandu nodded. "I think that's what she would like us to call him. Right, Seema?"

"Get back to work you, guys." Seema maintained a calm tone, although she was getting antsy by the minute. She was eager to see him, and she could not explain why.

There was no denying that she had developed a deep admiration for the man, and it was slowly turning into an obsession. Maybe she should just express her thoughts to him in the form of compliments, so she could get them off her mind and get him out of her mind.

It had been over a week since she spoke to him at the campsite, and the fire that he had ignited inside her burned stronger than the one outside. What happened that weekend that changed how she thought about him?

Was she just fascinated by how perfect he was? A stunningly gorgeous and caring man. Perfect for her.

"No. Stop it."

"What?" Jai and Nandu asked in unison over the headset, and that's when she realized she had spoken out loud.

"Oh, it's nothing."

"You okay, Seema? You seem lost," Jai asked.

"I think I can guess what this is about." Nandu raised her eyebrow high, looking at Seema. Nandu had always been doubtful about her choice to hire a private investigator.

"It's not what you think, Nandu. I am thinking of the main events."

Nandu let out a chuckle. "And I can't wait to see what Neeraj designed for all of us to wear at the wedding."

"Me, too." Seema smiled.

Jai interjected. "The eagle has landed, and so has her fiancé and her darling brother, the one and only Brozilla."

"Let's get this party started," Seema cheered.

Hours passed, and the group was not ready to simmer down. There was a planned cake- cutting to celebrate the one-year anniversary of Riya and her fiancé, Deepak, meeting at a friend's wedding.

Seema cleared her throat before speaking into her earpiece. "Guys, we need to tee up our chief guests to gather at the center of the dance floor. Who has eyes on Riya?"

No response.

"Where is Deepak?"

No response.

"Negative," Jai confirmed.

Seema heard Nandu giggle. "I don't see them either. Seema, relax. The young couple may be having a private moment."

Seema knew something was off. "Nandu or Jai, check with your teams if anyone has seen Riya."

A few minutes passed, and Jai finally spoke. "The caterer confirmed that the couple was seen going to the back of the building."

"I'm going to look for her. Find her brother for me. Something is off." Seema went down a utility elevator to the lowest level and stepped onto the grass at the back. She took two steps and stopped when she heard Riya's voice, and she did not sound happy. She knew she was not supposed to intervene, but she could not help herself. She turned the corner around the building and saw Riya standing with her back to the brick wall, and Deepak was looking at her, rage in his eyes.

"Riya, is everything okay?" Seema kept her eyes on the girl who refused to raise her eyes.

Deepak spoke before Riya could. "Seema, talk some sense into her."

"Deepak, please don't take that tone." Seema looked away from him to look at Riya. "Are you okay?"

"She has lost her mind. This is not even something we should be debating. Such a small thing."

"If it is so small, then you let it go, Deepak."

Deepak let out a growl and looked at Seema. "We have been going in circles for the past hour, and I am sick of it. If you don't convince your client to agree, you will not have a wedding to plan and no check to cash."

Seema glared at the young man and said, "Nothing is more important than my client's happiness." She looked away from him and at Riya. "I'll be here if you want me."

Riya shook her head. "Get me out of here. I'm done talking to this guy who wants to walk away from everything we have over one, like he said, *small* issue."

Seema took Riya's hand in her and said, "Let's go."

Riya sniffled as she left Deepak looking after her in shock as Seema led her to the other side of the building. Seema pressed into her earpiece and instructed one of her teammates to bring her a bottle of water to the back of the building.

Riya sat in silence on a half-built brick wall taking small sips of water. Seema stood by her, giving her client the space she needed. "Riya, whatever you'd like to do. Say it."

"Men can be so stupid. I don't get that what I do for work is a problem for his uncle's family." She sniffled, and Seema listened silently as Riya continued. "Apparently, one of my clients is his uncle's business rival, and I should drop their project because his uncle doesn't like it. And you see what he said? He is willing to cancel the wedding over this. I just don't get it."

"Deep breaths, Riya."

'I grew up in a house where men respect women for what they do. I design for so many of Raghav's competitors, and he tells me that I should give it my best no matter who the client is, and Deepak is the exact opposite."

Seema took a deep breath and said, "In your disappointment, you are mixing up Deepak's uncle's requirement as his. You chose him for a reason, and if he weren't anything like the men you grew up respecting, you would have never liked him."

Riya looked up at Seema. "So, do you think—"

Her voice was lost when they heard footsteps behind Seema. Deepak was out of breath as he stopped next to Seema, looking at Riya. "I'm sorry, sweetheart. I should not have said what I said. Nothing is more important to me than you. Nothing."

Riya glared at him as he kneeled in front of her, and he reached for her hand and slapped his cheek with her limp fingers. "I deserve a bashing because I made you cry. I'm sorry."

"Deepak—"

"I'm never going to tell you how to do your job because you are amazing at it."

Seema smiled and started walking away and heard Riya let out a sob before hugging her fiancé. She stopped when she saw Raghav walk across the lawn toward her. He stopped a foot away from her, his eyes wandering to where Deepak and Riya sat hugging each other at a distance.

"What's wrong? I was told to find you."

Seema turned back to look at the sweet couple before looking up into Raghav's eyes. "Your sister is falling in love with her fiancé, all over again."

He smiled. "And you know that, how?"

She blushed. "I saw it in her eyes."

"Really?" He stepped in front of her as she was about to walk away.

She tilted her chin and challenged the look in his eyes. "What?"

"What do my eyes tell you?"

She bit her lip. "That you are excited about the Sangeet ceremony, and you are still licking your wounds from last week's dance-off where you froze in the middle of the song."

She got a kick out of watching his jaw drop slightly and turned to walk away from him. His eyes were on her, and she knew it. A voice deep inside her challenged that she turn and look to see if he still had his eyes on her.

"No," she warned. But like her eyes had a mind of their own, they controlled her body as she turned to look in his direction to find him looking right at her.

Stop being silly, another voice scolded. You have a job to do.

Later that night, she was in the bathroom washing her face when Nandu came rushing in holding her phone. "*Brozilla* is calling you."

"Nandu, we talked about this." She took the phone from her and answered the call. "Hi, Raghav."

"Seema, so sorry to call you this late."

"Not a problem at all. How can I help?" Her lips curved up into a smile.

He fell silent for a few moments, and when he spoke, his voice was soft. "Thank you for being there for Riya."

Her heart melted for the man who took the time to call her. "It's part of my job."

"No. Don't oversimplify what you do. What you do is above and beyond what any event planner does. I see why Riya chose you to be the one to take care of her wedding, and I must say she made an excellent choice."

She batted away happy tears. "How is she doing?"

He chuckled. "She is great, and I've never seen her so happy."

"I'm so glad to hear that, and I cannot wait for the big event. Big one for you, too." She laughed.

"I don't know about that. Someone said I was still licking my wounds from my loss last weekend."

She blushed. "Don't listen to what those people tell you. You did amazingly well, and I cannot wait to see you dance with your sister."

"Me, too."

"Take care, I will talk to you later."

"Good night." She ended the call and kept looking at herself in the mirror.

The smile on her face seemed to be perpetual lately, and she shook her head at her image—the image of a person smiling off to glory—the undying goofy smile. Where did that come from?

12

"Raise your hand if you are ready for this." Riya laughed, pointing at the two rolling closets filled with wedding outfits for her and her family. The small group of family members who were gathered cheered enthusiastically.

"Me, too," Neeraj called out, making the entire group laugh.

Seema accompanied Neeraj and his team for the dress rehearsals with Riya's family. The large living area was occupied by close family members, and once Riya was done with her fittings, then her parents and other family members were to dress up and take pictures that would be used during the wedding for display purposes.

Riya was bouncing with energy with every trip to one of the bedrooms that were designated as the fitting room. Halfway through the outfit trials, Seema saw a beautiful, deep purple outfit made out of silk. The intricate threadwork was a bright pink making the outfit look dreamy and magical. She smiled, remembering a similar outfit she had seen at the boutique in a different color combination.

"Neeraj, how come Riya isn't trying on this outfit?" she asked.

"That's not for Riya." Neeraj brushed away her question.

"What? This is so beautiful. Why aren't you letting Riya have it? Don't tell me you made this for another client."

Neeraj pressed his fingers to his temple. "This outfit was not supposed to be here. It made it here accidentally."

"Okay. Big deal. Have Riya try it on."

"No. It's a special order for someone else." Neeraj shook his head.

Seema narrowed her eyes at him. "You were supposed to work on Riya's outfits exclusively. And now you tell me you took a special order?"

"Seema, please. Can we talk about it later?"

"Sure, but I need to know who you made this for? Another client?"

Neeraj looked at her for a long moment. "This outfit was ordered for you."

"What? By whom?"

Neeraj shook his head. "This is not how it was supposed to go."

"Neeraj?"

"Riya's brother's assistant called and put in the special order for you."

"You are kidding." She glared at him.

"No. I was told to make the dress and deliver it with Riya's clothes. Now I need to attend to Riya."

"Fine. Go. I will deal with you later." She let out a growl before stepping out of the room to process the information she heard from the designer. She stepped onto the balcony that was off of the living area and took out her phone to text Raghav.

Seema: *WE NEED TO TALK.*

Raghav: *Hi Seema. Your caps lock is on. J*

She let out a huffed breath.

Seema: *Mr. Vasudev. We need to talk now, please.*

She stared at the phone as the three dots danced indicating he was typing a response.

Raghav: *At the gym. Top floor. Take the elevator to the fourth floor.*

She looked around the house and saw the elevator to one side of the house. She discretely walked through the elevator doors and rode up to the top floor, her mind a whirlwind of questions.

Why was such an expensive outfit ordered for her?

She stepped out of the elevator and stopped to take in the view on the top floor. The mini sanctuary of plants she had seen outside Raghav's place was recreated throughout the floor with a different kind of seating areas set up all around the open terrace.

"Seema," she heard him call out to her from the other end of the space from an area designated as the gym.

Her heart started to thud when their eyes met as he stood by the glass doors in a t-shirt and shorts wiping away sweat with a towel.

"Are you okay?"

She let out a sigh. "I'm... I need to know why Mrs. Sharma put in an order for an outfit for me."

A sly smile played on his lips. "I guess you should ask Mrs. Sharma then."

"Raghav, this is not funny."

"I'm not laughing. You will need to ask Mrs. Sharma." He turned to walk away from her, and on instinct, she stepped in front of him.

"Would you please call Mrs. Sharma? I don't have her phone number."

He shook his head. "Not now. I'm busy. I need to get back to my workout."

She lowered her eyes and let out a sigh, not knowing how to deal with the situation. This is one such scenario she had not experienced in all the years she had managed weddings. He stood in front of her in silence for a long moment before speaking. "What's wrong?"

She raised her eyes to his. "Would Mrs. Sharma order a designer outfit for me without your knowledge?"

"I was made aware, and it was Riya's idea to get you a gift."

"Why?"

"She wanted to say thank you for everything you have been doing for her." His voice was soft yet casual.

"Mr. Vasudev, this is highly unprofessional and unacceptable."

"Why is that?" He raised a curious eyebrow.

"Do you buy your employees at your offices or factories clothes?"

He folded his arms in front of him. "There is something called a bonus program for folks who work harder than the others."

"Do you buy them designer outfits?"

"I don't. But I can see why Riya chose this route. It's a form of bonus." He kept a calm tone.

"This is not fair. Where is the bonus for the rest of my team? They worked harder than I did for all the events."

"What's your point, Seema?"

"It was inappropriate for you to pay for an outfit for me."

He looked at her for a long moment. "Riya told me she saw you admiring that outfit when you were at the boutique. She wanted you to have it."

She held his gaze. "Fine. I'll take it if you let me pay you for it."

"Are you for real? Why can't you accept a token of appreciation?"

"I... I cannot and—" Her voice was lost when she saw that Mr. Sangha was calling. "Excuse me. I need to take this call. We still need to talk."

He threw his hands up as she turned away and answered the call. She turned to look at him, her eyes scorching him for his inappropriate behavior, but that very look only made him smile.

"She wants to pay me for the dress?" he scoffed as his eyes followed her as she stepped into the outdoor space speaking on the phone.

Raghav kept his eyes on her as she sat down on one of the chairs, and just the way she grabbed the armrest, he knew something was wrong. He saw her press her fingers to her temple, and at that moment, the woman who was demanding an explanation for his unprofessional behavior looked weak like something came crashing on her.

His mind told him to give let her be since she walked away to take the call, but something deep inside, something primal, told him he needed to go to her. And before he could debate about the best course of action, he was moving toward her. He watched her end the call and look up at the sky as she took in a deep breath like she was fighting a great sorrow.

Raghav didn't know how she would react to him being around her when she was in a sad state, but he could not get himself to leave, not knowing what the cause of the gloom in her eyes was. He stopped a foot away trying to get a read on her, and when he heard her sniffle, something twisted in his chest. The next instant, he was on his knees by her side.

He slowly placed his hand on her knee and asked, "What's wrong?"

She shook her head but could not suppress the sob that escaped her.

Raghav slowly reached out and took her hand in his. "You can scold me later for not being professional and intrude into your personal matters, but I can't walk away when you look so sad. How can I help?"

"Just tell me I have been stupid to believe I have a family out there and that I need to stop looking." She blinked away tears as she looked away from him.

"Seema, was that your client who was working on the DNA research?"

She looked at him, surprised. "You remember?"

He nodded. "What happened to the research?"

She took in a deep breath. "No match. Millions of DNA samples and no match whatsoever."

"We have seven billion people in the world, and you are going to stop looking because you didn't find a match in the first few million?"

She looked at him for a long moment. "Don't say that. I will spend the rest of my life doing this and hoping to find a family."

He shrugged. "If that's what you want to do, go for it. Wouldn't you rather do that than repent later about not doing something about it, especially when you know, deep inside, that's what you want to do."

She nodded. "It's heartbreaking every time I get a negative result, but I cannot get myself to stop. Nandu thinks it's because of—" She stopped like she realized she was about to open up to him again just like she did at the campsite.

"Because?" he prompted.

Seema shook her head. "Thank you for talking to me."

"Why are you doing that again?" he asked.

"What?"

"Finish your thought."

"I... I shouldn't. It's not appropriate."

"Really? Why?" His tone held mockery as he added, "You taking the blame when Riya was emotional was appropriate, you being there for her when she had the toughest time with her fiancé was acceptable, but I can't help out?"

"No. It's not the same."

"I've never seen you as someone Riya employed for a job because you have been more than a friend to her. From what I can see, you will be a good friend of our family after the wedding. So, stop being difficult and tell me how I can help with what is going on."

She shook her head. "I can't believe I am having this conversation with you."

"Yes, you are, and I am going to tell you, you need to listen to your heart. No matter what people around you say, they are your well-wishers, but no one knows you better than yourself."

"Nandu is very supportive, but she is under the impression that I am doing this search because my ex told me he could not have a future with someone like me who didn't know my background, but I want to do it for myself. I want to know what my parents and grandparents did even if they are still around."

"Then you should do it. Why would you stop?"

She shook her head. "I think I have exhausted all my options. If they could not find a DNA match from the state where I grew up and all the surrounding states in the northern part, where else should I look?"

He thought for a moment. "As I said, you shouldn't stop because a few million DNA samples didn't find a good match. There are seven billion people out there, you should at least check a billion."

She managed to smile. "Right. Should I start looking in Italy because I like pizza?"

He thought for a moment. "You grew up in the northern part of India, but when I saw you for the first time, I placed you as someone from the south. Have you looked around the area where you are?"

"No. I don't have any link to this area. I moved here for my job."

He nodded. "You know, people tend to gravitate toward their roots knowingly or unknowingly, and if there are other locations that you need to start looking, they are the places you find the most happiness in. It could be any place."

"I can't think of another place, but I chose this city over another town, and maybe I should start looking around me."

"There you go." He smiled.

She wiped the edge of her eyes and said, "Thank you. I appreciate you talking to me."

"Good. Will you accept the dress Neeraj made for you as a 'you are welcome' gift?"

She narrowed her eyes. "No. Unacceptable."

He looked at her for a long moment. "You should have it."

"I'm sorry. I cannot accept gifts."

"Fine. Riya is not in the habit of taking back gifts, either." He stood up and stepped away from her.

"Fine, then." She walked past him and stopped when he called out to her.

"Forget about who paid for it. Accept the gift. Riya will be very happy."

"Why?" Her voice was a whisper.

He shook his head as he stepped closer to her. "For all the happiness you give people around you, you deserve everything you wish for."

"Thank you," she said and walked away from him. Yet again, she felt his eyes on her with his words resonating in her ears.

You deserve everything you ever wish for.

What if her heart wished for him, a man like him who could fill the void in her life with his love and care? Will that come true?

13

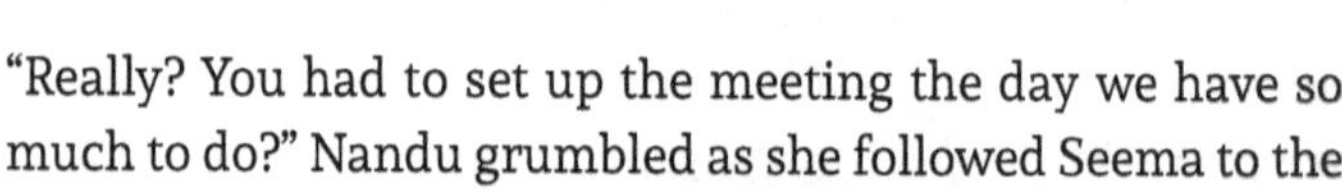

"Really? You had to set up the meeting the day we have so much to do?" Nandu grumbled as she followed Seema to the lobby of the Janatha Seva Party office building.

"Nandu, remember we set this appointment weeks back. I didn't have Riya's final walkthrough scheduled for this day. We pushed it out so Raghav could attend."

"Brozilla again."

"Nandu," Seema warned.

"Fine. I'm sure you are madly in love with him because he said you should continue the search, and you hate me for asking you to stop."

Seema stopped and turned to look at her friend. "I don't love him or hate you. I thought it was good advice, and I knew he was being objective when he told me I should do whatever would make me happy."

"Whatever." Nandu rolled her eyes.

"Hey, let me tell you that I could not have gotten over every failed investigation if I didn't have you."

"Yeah, yeah, sure." Nandu smiled as they started walking toward the front desk.

"We are here to meet Mr. Sravan. I have an appointment."

The person behind the front desk checked on the computer and said, "I don't see an appointment. And Mr.

Sravan is busy at that time."

Seema smiled. "There must be a mistake." She showed her phone screen with the text from Sravan confirming the appointment time.

The person behind the desk looked at the date on the text message and said, "Oh, this was before our new system was set up. And unfortunately, Sravan sir is in a meeting with his brother."

Seema nodded. "I understand. Can you give me another appointment for later today or tomorrow?"

The man shook his head. "I am so sorry, I don't have any openings."

Seema thought for a moment. "Since I have his phone number, can I text and ask him directly? Will you add it to his calendar if he agrees to a time?"

"Absolutely."

Seema pulled up the old conversation she had with Sravan over text and sent him a message.

Seema: *Seema here, we spoke a few weeks back. I am here for our appointment to discuss the anniversary party, and I understand, but there has been a mix-up. Please let me know if you have another time this week to meet? Thank you!*

She hit send and looked at the man behind the desk. "Would you please give me your contact info, so I can call when Sravan sir confirms the time?"

"Sure—" The man was about to give her the number when his desk phone rang, and he excused himself to answer it. "Yes, sir. She is here. Definitely."

Seema smiled, liking the timing of the phone call and the sound of it. "Was that Sravan sir?"

"Yes. He would like to meet with you now." The man smiled and gave them instructions to his office on the upper level of the building.

"That was nice of Mr. Sravan." Nandu smiled as they went up the stairs to his office.

The door to the office they were headed to opened as they got closer, and a young man stepped out. "Seema, I'm so sorry about the mix-up."

"No problem, sir. This is Nandini, my Production Manager."

"Sravan, please. Nice to meet you both. Please come. My brother is here as well, so it is a perfect time to discuss the services you provide for event management." He led them into the office where another man was seated. "Seema and Nandini, this is my older brother, Varun."

"Nice to meet you." Varun smiled.

"Likewise, sir." Seema smiled.

"Varun, please. We are not formal around here."

"Sure." Seema placed her business portfolio on the table and said, 'Why don't we share our experience with event management, and you can tell us what you had in mind for your weekend events."

Seema and Nandu spent the next twenty minutes taking turns walking the brothers through the various events they had organized for other clients and spent time understanding their event needs for the anniversary party.

After noting the details, Seema was happy with the conversation they had. "Mr. Sravan, I mean Sravan and Varun, we will work on a proposal for the next few events with the associated cost in a few days, and we can take it from there."

"Sounds good." Sravan nodded.

"Thank you, I will be sure to get time on your calendar for our next meeting."

Sravan shook his head. "Not necessary. You have my phone number. Call or text when you are ready, and I will make time."

"I appreciate that very much, and we truly believe in Mr. Rayudu's leadership." Seema was encouraged by the level of detail the brothers shared with her.

"Thank you. We hope to bring the much-needed change."

Seema and Nandini left, and Varun kept looking at the portfolio they had left behind.

"What are you thinking about, brother?" Sravan asked.

"Why does Seema look so familiar? Have you worked with her before?" Varun flipped through the folder with the event pictures.

"I haven't, but maybe you have. Secretly planning a wedding, huh?" Sravan laughed.

"Stop kidding. I'm serious. Why is that woman so familiar?"

"Maybe you saw her at one of the weddings you attended."

"Possibly."

Sravan interjected, "I know why she is familiar. She looks just like Anu auntie's daughter."

Varun scrunched his nose. "Who?"

"Ma's first cousin who lives in Singapore." Sravan pulled up his phone and showed the social media image of the teenager.

Varun smiled. "I can see the similarity except for the purple hair."

"Right." Varun laughed and added, "I think we should plan sooner rather than later."

"Okay. I will take care of it. I'll see you for dinner. Ma wants us both home this evening." Varun reminded.

"See you later, brother."

*****

"I need a break now." Riya collapsed on the backrest of the chair, feigning a faint after running through the step-by-step plan of her entry and subsequent steps through the main events that were planned in the week.

"We can take a break, but we need one final run-through. We will be back in thirty minutes." Seema smiled at Riya and nodded at her team leads who were there for the event review.

Riya's mother stood up from the table where they were sitting. "I will send snacks for you all while you relax."

"Thank you, Mrs. Vasudev." Seema smiled.

Riya got up from her chair. "I will be right back as well."

The key family members left, leaving Seema and her team at the table. Seema looked at Jai and asked, "How are the performances coming along? Do we need any other practices?"

Jai shook his head. "Didn't you just say we were all on a break?"

The group broke into laughter, and Seema smiled. "Riya is on a break. We aren't."

"I object. We are all on break."

"We all go on a break after—" Seema's voice was lost when she saw Riya walking back to the table with her grandmother and Raghav. Seema and her team stood up in respect to the elderly woman who had been so caring about Seema and her team. Seema had grown fond of the older woman from the moment she had stopped her in the middle of an event and asked if she and her team had eaten their meals. She had been sweet enough to make sure everyone on Seema's team was well fed at all times.

"You are all here." The older woman sat on one of the chairs, smiling at everyone.

"Good to see you, ma'am."

The older woman nodded. "I don't want to disturb your planning, but I wanted you all to have something from me. It is our family tradition to gift our family and friends new clothes for a girl's wedding, and I wanted to give them to you before you all get very busy."

Seema's eyes immediately went to Raghav's as he handed a paper bag to his grandmother. The older woman took the bag and handed it to Seema. "This is for you, my child, for the beautiful events you have put together."

"Thank you." Seema took the open-top bag, and one peek at the contents, she knew what her gift was. It was the outfit she had refused to accept from Raghav that he had managed to get her to accept from his grandmother.

Sneaky. Sneaky but cute.

She looked around at the happy faces of her teammates receiving the gifts, and she knew there was no way for her to push back on what was gifted to her. She wasn't going to do that to Riya's grandmother.

"This is very generous of you. Thank you." Nandu smiled.

"It was Riya and Raghav's idea. They are the ones to thank."

Seema kept her eyes on him as he modestly declined the idea being his and that all the credit should go to his sister. The team thanked her for the gifts and left the table as if to catch a break from Seema, leaving her with Riya, Raghav, and their grandmother.

"Next, I want to see my grandson married." The older woman hugged Raghav.

Riya let out a laugh. "That day may be sooner than you think, Nani."

"Really?" Riya's mother asked as she came to join them.

Raghav let out a scoff. "What are you doing, Riya?"

"Nothing. But I am very excited for you, brother," Riya teased, and Seema found an opportune moment to seek some revenge for his persistence to get her and her team gifts even after she had told him she could not accept gifts.

"Riya, is that why you asked me to keep my calendar free in a year?" Seema smiled at Raghav, and he narrowed his eyes at his sister.

"Raghav, are you not planning to invite us to your wedding?"

"Maybe he will elope like his grandfather." His grandmother laughed.

"Don't you dare," his mother warned her son as she placed the snacks on the table.

"Ma, cut it out. Riya, I will deal with you later."

His mother tsked. "I don't know why you are being so secretive."

"By the way, Ma, I think he shared the special dish you sent to his place with her." Riya giggled, and Raghav rolled his eyes.

"Raghav, how is it that Riya knows all this?"

Raghav shot one look at Seema when he realized she was the one to add fuel to the fire. "Yes, Ma. I shared the dessert you made for me with her. She loved it very much."

Seema let out a low gasp, worried he was going to reveal the secret dance practice to save himself from the grilling. "Riya, we can get back to the planning if you are ready."

Raghav interjected. "Let's wait for the team to get back, Seema. Let me also tell my mom that the woman I met that night licked the dessert bowl clean."

Seema blushed and hoped no one noticed her dying need to hide under the table.

"So, she came to your apartment?"

He nodded. "She may have been in the apartment when you came to drop off the dessert."

"What? And you didn't introduce me to her. That's rude." Riya was suddenly pissed.

"Excuse me." Seema stood up to escape the conversation she knew was going to get torturous, but she only wanted to get away.

"Oh, Seema, you should stay. I might even give you some dates you can block on your calendar," he stated, making her force a smile.

"Who is this woman?" Riya demanded.

Raghav winked. "Someone who thought your black wall was a brilliant idea and that I should let you redo my entire place."

"I like her already," Riya said cheerfully.

"Yeah?"

"Raghav, you better not be joking." His mother looked confused.

"I'm not, Ma. This woman exists. She is smart, caring, hardworking, and very down to earth."

Seema kept her eyes on the sheets of printed paper as if she were not listening, but her heart thudded in her chest. She could not get herself to look up at him as he continued to sing her praises.

"He is joking, Riya. He is just describing his ideal woman. We should not fall for his tricks." His mother laughed, leaving the room, and Riya followed to make a phone call. The room fell silent as Seema pretended to be looking at her phone, not wanting to make eye contact with him.

Raghav's grandmother was the one to break the silence. "Raghav, I don't know if you were joking or not, but the last few weeks you have looked so happy. I used to see you stressed all the time, but now, I see you spending time with us and being just happy. I even heard you humming the other day. Are you sure you are not in love?"

Seema's heart started to thud, and all she could think about was to become invisible. She didn't know why her heart raced like it was going to leap out of her chest.

He laughed, relief sweeping over her. "Nani, you've been watching way too many Bollywood movies lately."

"You just don't know yet, silly." The older woman smiled.

"Sure, Nani. Let's see if I will get to know anytime soon. I'm surely impressed with the woman, and she doesn't take compliments or tokens of appreciation well."

His words made her smile which she kept hidden behind the computer screen. She looked away when her phone buzzed.

Raghav: *Having fun, are we?*

Seema: *I always have fun while planning weddings.*

Raghav: *I'm sure you had a lot more fun adding fuel to the fire Riya set off.*

Seema: *Me? I was just making sure why Riya wanted me to block my calendar.*

Raghav: *So, you busy blocking your calendar then?*

Seema: *Do you want me to?*

Raghav: *I don't know yet. I'll tell you when I'm ready.*

Her heart started to thud again. What is he talking about now?

Raghav: *I'm busy with my factory reconstruction.*

Seema: *Oh, repairs from the fire accident?*

Raghav: *That and also expansion.*

Seema: *What do you make in the factory?*

Raghav: *Depends on the type of client. Mostly electronic components that are used for medical equipment.*

Seema: *Oh, the one you have a patent on?*

Raghav: *Someone did their research.*

Seema: *I saw the patent certificates when I was at your parents' house. I am curious to see what happens in a factory. Can a visitor get a tour?*

Raghav: *I could arrange something. When do you want to go? This week?*

Seema: *Sorry, I'm in the middle of an event. How about the week after Riya's wedding?*

Raghav: *Sure. Can you check with Kamala ma'am and set up a time? You can ask her why she ordered the dress for you when you speak to her.*

Seema bit her lip not wanting him to catch her smiling.

Seema: *I have figured out why she ordered the dress for me.*

Raghav: *Good you did.*

Seema: *I will be sure to thank her.*

Raghav: *Please do.*

Seema: *If I may, I would like to get back to my current client's event.*

"Have fun, you guys." Raghav left the room, and Seema raised her eyes to look at him as he walked away.

"Thank you," she called out, and that made him stop before turning to look at her.

"Thank you!" he emphasized, making her heart flutter with joy.

14

"That's it for the night. All the guests in the wedding party are all checked in." Nandu placed her headset on the table in the large room that Seema and her team took over as the control center for the event. Seema and her team arrived a few days prior at the resort to get everything set up for the weekend wedding with the major events lined up back to back.

"Good. Please ensure we have extra security covering all employee entrances as well. We cannot have any paparazzi enter the building."

"That's taken care of."

"Go get some sleep." Seema patted her best friend's shoulder.

"You're the one who needs to sleep most."

Seema winked. "I'll start sleeping on Sunday evening."

"Don't start your zombie phase yet." Nandu laughed.

"I'll be fine. Go sleep."

"Good night. Jai is in the banquet hall practicing the dance." Nandu yawned as she left the room.

Seema was running through the checklist one last time for the day when she heard a knock on the door. She looked up to find Raghav at the door, looking as gorgeous as ever even though he was only wearing a t-shirt and cargo shorts. She had not seen him in a week but had thought of him every moment. Every single thing she did reminded her of him, and he was on her mind all the time.

"Hi, Raghav."

"Would you care for a drink?" he asked as he stood by the door.

"No. I'm good. Thank you."

He turned away from her and gestured to someone before he stepped into the room. "What are you working on?"

She placed her pencil on the table as he sat across from her. "The usual stuff."

"There is nothing usual about what you do."

She smiled. "Thank you. How was your business trip?"

"Someone is keeping tabs on me." He chuckled.

"I called Mrs. Sharma as you suggested to make an appointment for my factory tour, and she mentioned you were out on a last-minute trip."

"So, you're serious about visiting the factory?"

"Why wouldn't I be? I can't wait." She shrugged.

"I thought you were busy supporting the events for the newly formed political party."

"We are still at the inception phase with the political events, and we would be providing basic services like catering and taking care of logistics. My core team and I get to catch a break."

"Okay, good. Hope you enjoy the tour."

"Sounds good." She smiled and leaned closer and whispered, "Are you ready for your dance tomorrow?"

He leaned closer, filling the space around her with his woody and masculine cologne and whispered back, "I don't know."

She let out a laugh, pulling back to look at him. "I think you are ready."

"So, the plan is to let Riya finish dancing with our cousin, and then I go join her?" he asked.

"Yes. The MCs script will say that there was a special request for an encore of the dance, and that's when you will join. We will pull Ravi back, so you can join."

"Good. I'm glad you are not canceling a high school kid's performance." He snickered.

She widened her eyes as if in horror. "We would never do that."

He nodded, smiling, his eyes holding hers in silence. "How are you doing?"

"I'm good. Excited for Riya."

"How is your research coming along?"

Her eyes brightened with joy. "You were right about broadening the search. There seems to be a DNA match with people in the neighboring region, less than two percent, but it's better than the no match I had in the earlier round."

"Good. My guess was right about you being from around here."

"Yeah, explains my obsession with a few things that are very regional."

"You look happy."

She nodded. "This is the first time in all these years I have a sliver of hope that I will actually get to know where my roots are, and even better, find a distant relative."

"What will you do when you find your relatives?"

She thought for a moment. "I have a ton of questions to ask them. Like the history of the family and stories... I love to hear about those old-time stories, and then I'm going to take a page out of your family and plan a reunion with all my relatives."

"That is some grand planning."

"There's got to be some advantage of having an event planner as a relative." She laughed and added, "When I find them."

"I wish you luck, and if you don't find all your relatives in the next few months, you should join us for our family reunion."

"What? Are you serious?"

"Yeah."

"That's it. You can't take it back. I'm definitely going." She laughed.

He shook his head. "That's what I said. You should go with us."

"You are messing with me."

"I'm serious."

"And the reunion will be in that house that was in the picture?"

"Yes." He smiled, one end of his mouth twisting up.

"That place is so beautiful. I can't believe we didn't have an event at the house. It would have been awesome."

"Not a unique enough venue for your client, I guess," he teased.

"No. It's the logistics and accommodating all the guests. It would make such a beautiful venue for an intimate wedding." She smiled dreamily.

"My grandparents had their celebration at the house after they eloped and came back."

Seema's eyes widened. "I have been dying to hear about that story. Why did they elope?"

"If you want to hear all the stories, you will need to spend weeks with my family, and they get super fun after that because they start to repeat, and you hear other versions of the story."

Seema let out a sigh. "I really want to go now. Would you please let me organize it for you?"

He shook his head, laughing. "I told you that you could go. You don't need to work the event."

She scrunched her nose. "I can't crash a family event."

"Yes, you can."

"No. It's not appropriate for me to attend a family event."

He rolled his eyes. "Oh, you forgot to mention, unprofessional."

"That, too. It's sweet of you to invite me, but I can't."

"Why? Why are you such a stickler for rules? Rules that you made."

She shrugged, looking away from him.

"What's with the formalities and such rules? Your team is a lot more easy-going about the *sir and ma'am* part but not you."

"It's the best way." A lump started to form in her throat at the harsh reality around why she set those rules for herself.

"Best way for what?" he prompted.

She lowered her eyes and fell silent.

"Seema, talk to me."

She looked up and took a deep breath. "The first wedding I worked, I was fascinated with the family dynamics, and I very quickly got too attached. Got too involved with the family to the point where I forgot I was the hired help. When all the fun comes to an end, the harsh reality hits me harder than anyone else because I don't have a family of my own. That's why I insist on the formalities and look what you and your sister have done. I'm going to have a family hangover for months now."

Raghav looked at her for a long moment feeling the tightness in his chest increase, and for the first time in many years, he didn't know what to do. How is it that the most beautiful person inside and out has such a void in her life when she was the life of the party, the catalyst to everyone's happiness. The twist in his chest was suffocating, and as if it were the only way to create a distraction for both of them, he said, "I think I need one last round of practice."

She smiled, making the weight in his chest lift a bit. "I think we should, just so you burn the floor down with your moves."

He was glad to see the spark return to her eyes, but the twist only tightened as he started dancing with her. The woman was putting on a strong front but was all alone on the inside with a beautiful heart that brought happiness to others.

As he looked at her and watched her dance, he knew he would do anything to keep that spark alive, forever. The past few months were the most interesting ones in his life, and it only made him wonder what it would be like to have someone like her for the rest of his life.

Life would be beautiful.

15

"Don't be nervous. You got this," Seema whispered as she stood next to Raghav the following night, watching the youngest performers on stage.

"Don't say that. I'm not nervous."

"You look nervous." She smiled.

"What?"

"You adjusted your tie eighty-three thousand times, you pulled on your cuffs seventeen times, and you ran your fingers through your hair so many times, all the styling is gone."

"I hated what the guy did to my hair."

She bit her lip. "I have to agree, your hair looks better this way."

"Oh, good. You like my messy hair."

She looked up at him. "My liking doesn't matter. I only said that the natural look suits you."

"Whatever. For the record, you ruined this event for me."

"I'm sorry you feel that way, Mr. Vasudev, but the bride is our focus today, so please suck it up and put on a good show for your lovely sister."

"Yes, I will, Ms. Seema Kumar."

She let out a laugh. "You'll be fine, Raghav."

"That's the Seema I like. The other one called me *Brozilla.*"

"I did not. Never."

He chuckled. "Definitely not to my face."

"You are making me nervous now. Please stop."

He laughed victoriously. "Mission accomplished."

"What happens if I pull out now."

She turned to look at him, perplexed. "You will not."

"I won't, not after you spent all that time teaching me."

"You are doing this for Riya, remember that."

"For Riya."

"Absolutely. She is the bride, and she gets everything her way."

"I'm the bride's brother. What do I get?" he teased.

"You get to dance with the bride."

"How come you don't dance? I know you love to dance."

She smiled, lowering her eyes for a moment before looking up at him. "This is a family event, and our job is to teach the family members to perform for the bride and groom. It's no fun if we dance, right?"

He fell silent as they watched the show from backstage. Riya and Deepak cheered and hooted for their family members who were performing for them. What started off with the youngest members of the family, followed with the oldest, ended with the grandparents doing a coordinated dance with their arms from where they were seated.

The event was coming together beautifully, especially with the last-minute change they could make to recreate the stage based on the wall theme that Riya had created at Raghav's place. The black background with antique lamps in bronze and teal blue hung from the top, and multiple levels caused a mysterious yet fun aspect on the stage.

"The setup is beautiful," he said, clapping for the performers.

"I'm so glad Nandu was able to pull it off."

"Yes, she did. Do you think Riya managed to figure out the mystery woman I shared my mom's dessert with was you?"

She turned around to look at him. "How can she do that? Did you tell her?"

"No. But I told her the mystery woman liked the wall."

"As long as it doesn't ruin her surprise, I'm good with that."

"Your obsession with surprises is unbelievable."

"Who doesn't love a good surprise? I would love to have surprises in my life every day, but I get more of the shocks and curveballs." She laughed.

"Would it be a surprise if I didn't dance tonight?" He laughed.

"You are dancing tonight. I will stand right here and show you the moves as you are doing them."

"How about I go say hi to a few of the guests and come back here? Maybe that'll ease your nervousness."

"No. I'm not nervous. Please stay. Don't go."

"You are a bad liar." He let out a laugh.

"Okay, remember not to step on Riya's dress when she twirls."

He looked at his sister and the beautiful magenta dress she was wearing. "That thing looks like I could get killed if I slipped and fell under it."

"Very funny. It's an incredibly beautiful dress."

"Wasn't this the one you picked out for her when we were held hostage at the boutique?"

Seema smiled. "It's perfect for her."

"I need a drink. I'll be right back."

She reached out and held him by his elbow. "I'll get you what you want. Just stay put."

"Nice. I didn't know that was an option."

She pressed into her earpiece and asked one of her teammates to have a drink sent for Raghav.

"Do you think I'm gonna run to evade the performance?"

She shook her head. "I don't know. I don't know you well enough to guess your behavior, so I am going to keep an eye on you."

"That's some commitment."

"We take our jobs very seriously around here." Her eyes glowed with pride.

"So, I take it that you have security watching me as well."

She blushed. "We always have one-on-one coverage from security for the key family members."

Raghav looked around the space and pointed at a young man who stood to one side. "Let me guess, that man is my assigned security."

"Maybe."

He let out a laugh. "Look at me, Seema. Do I look like I need security? I can be that man's security."

She smiled, not choosing to respond to his question because he was right. Raghav was tall and well-built with lean muscle. He stood by her, making her look tiny. The suit jacket he had on for the night fit him like a glove and had heads turning as he walked through the aisles greeting their guests.

She had only recently started noticing the various emotions in his eyes, and neither of them readable. His smile was ever gorgeous, and every time their eyes meet, she has a strange excitement course through her. The more she ignored it, the stronger it got, but she knew the moment she stopped seeing him, she would forget.

It was part of the family hangover she had managed very well for years until this wedding. She would be hungover every single person in the family, especially the bride's brother.

"Riya is up next, and we cannot find Ravi, anywhere," Nandu sounded frantic.

"Track him down. Don't we have the tracking beacon set on his jacket?" Seema asked.

"I found him." Relief swept over Seema when she heard Jai's voice.

"Good, bring him. He is up next."

"Seema, I don't know if he should dance. He has been drinking from his grandpa's glass all evening."

"How did this happen? How could we let a minor drink?"

Jai chuckled. "Apparently, he turned eighteen two days ago, and his cool grandfather has been letting him sip the good stuff all evening."

"What do we do?"

Jai chuckled. "Plan B was to have Riya perform solo. We can have her switch to a solo dance."

"No. Let's do the partner one." She turned to look at Raghav who stood watching the show unaware of the conversations going on over the walkie-talkie.

"Who will dance with her?" Jai asked.

"Tee it up, the bride's brother is going to dance with her. No change in announcements. Stick to the plan. Swap out the partner."

"Oh my God. You actually got him to agree to dance?" Nandu was overjoyed.

"And practiced, too," she said and turned to look at Raghav. "You are up next."

"Wait. Ravi needs to go first."

She pressed her lips. "Ravi is attending a different version of the Sangeet party. Twenty-one-year-old whiskey in an eighteen-year-old's tummy."

"Nice! That kid knows what to drink."

"Okay, you ready?"

"Am I ready? What do you think?" He laughed.

"You got this, Raghav. You are handsome and stunning when you dance."

He chuckled. "Really, how come you didn't tell me this before?"

"Let's go." She kept her eyes on Riya as the MC announced her dance with 'Her Brother' when the family was expecting her to dance with her cousin.

Seema held her breath as Riya took the steps to the stage, a team member lifting the heavy hem of the dress for her to walk onto the stage. Her heart started to thud when the music came on, and Riya started her solo fifteen seconds before her partner was to enter. She scanned the guests and noticed they all had their eyes on the bride, but Seema locked her peripheral vision on her brother.

She turned when it was time and mouthed *go* to Raghav, and he smiled before looking away to step on the stage, his long legs giving him a smooth entry. The crowd cheered loudly, but Seema waited for the moment when Riya would turn and realize she was about to dance with her brother, something she never imagined would happen.

The moment happened, and it was magical. Seema's eyes blurred when Riya let out a squeal of joy that was heard over the loud music. She looked to her team, who was looking at the performance in blissful shock.

The bride laughed in sheer joy as she danced, and her brother followed the choreography to a tee. If the expression on the bride's face was priceless, there were no words to describe the joy in the family members' eyes, especially for the grandparents, who relished the sight of their grandkids dancing for the first time ever.

She kept her eyes on Riya, overjoyed to see her client's happiness as she danced with her brother. There was a moment when she looked away from Riya and at Raghav, and at that very moment, he looked at her, and their eyes locked. Time stood still.

What she saw in his eyes, she had no words to describe, but her heart responded to the unspoken words, and it drummed a parade in her chest, deafening her. Her breath was caught in her throat, and all she could remember was how beautiful his scent was when he was close, and her skin tingled like it remembered the warmth that she experienced when he stood close to her.

She looked away, unable to get a handle on the turmoil that brewed inside her. She was out of breath as if she had been running for miles. The loud applause cut through the sound of her beating heart, and she looked up to find the happy siblings take a bow. She clapped, laughing even as tears rolled down her cheeks just like they did with almost every one of the family and friends who witnessed the beautiful performance.

She watched as Raghav whispered something in Riya's ear as he looked at her, and the next instant, Riya called out, "Seema, I love you."

Seema took deep breaths to find the overwhelming joy Riya's words brought to her. She watched as Raghav took the microphone and addressed the group who was gathered as Riya's parents joined the siblings on the stage.

"I hope you all enjoyed Riya's beautiful dance, and I'm sure you tolerated me being on the stage with her. We are very happy that you were able to join us tonight, and I want to take a moment to thank the team who made this and every other prior event happen." He paused and looked around the open space at Seema's team and said, "Guys,

I cannot thank you enough for all your efforts. You have made every moment special for us, and we will treasure these memories forever, and a special thanks to the woman who created a moment for Riya and me to share forever, Seema. Thank you, you are the best!!"

Nandu walked over to where Seema stood shaking and hugged her. "You are just the bomb. This was such a wonderful surprise. Brozilla dancing with his sister. Nothing beats that."

The crowd broke into a clamor, and the DJ took over, inviting everyone to join in while Seema took the opportunity to take a moment to gather herself. The kind words the family said to her touched her deep inside and threatened to fill the abyss of loneliness she thought could never be done.

She took off her headset and ran toward the back of the stage and plastered her back to the wall as she caught her breath. Tears of joy rolled down her cheeks while the affectionate words played in her ears. What hit her most was the look Raghav had in his eyes like she was the world to him.

Was she imagining that?

If she wasn't, she wanted what she thought she could never have. *Him.* Him alone would fill the void she had all her life.

16

"Seema," Raghav's voice cut through her haze, and she looked in his direction as he walked toward her.

She wiped the edge of her eyes and looked away like she didn't want him to see her in this vulnerable state. "Hey."

"Seema, why are you here?" He stopped less than a foot from her and waited for a few moments. When she kept her eyes lowered, he stepped closer to her and gently raised her chin with his finger. "What's wrong?"

She blinked away the tears and looked at him. "It was beautiful. Thank you for your kind words."

He smirked. "You know why it was beautiful? Because you poured your heart and soul into everything. I don't know if I would have thought of doing something like this for my own family. You made the magic happen tonight. The tears of joy, the undying smiles, and the hearts filled with endless happiness, you were the reason for it all. That beautiful heart of yours has only known to give and not take. Time for you to accept the affection and not question it."

She smiled, taking in the intensity of the moment as they looked into each other's eyes. "I guess I will have to learn to accept it and not question it."

A distant pop from a firework cut through the moment they shared, and she lowered her eyes. "I should get back."

Seema's heart was still pounding when she made it back to the main event area and saw almost all of the guests were on the dance floor, including her team. She blinked, unable to believe that her team leads and a few others, had mingled with the marriage party and were having fun.

The look of joy on their faces brought warmth to her chest, and she let out a sigh of relief. Maybe she was too tight on her rules about mingling with the clients. Was Raghav right about her not being able to take the love she was getting from people around her?

Before she could think either way, she saw a man bolt toward the group on the dance floor, a camera in hand.

"Security. Stop him." She pointed at the man who was taking pictures of the party as he trotted around before being slammed to the ground and his camera confiscated.

"Please check all the other areas," she said to the security team as she saw the man being taken away. Good thing no other guests noticed him.

She scanned the area and then the dance floor and spotted Raghav immediately, his head inches over everyone else as he tried to waltz with his grandmother. Memories of the blissful moments surfaced, but the harsh reality of all the fun coming to an end in a couple of days was hard to forget.

She took a deep breath and told herself she could not change her ways because of one affectionate family who treated her team with respect. At the end of the day, they were still employees and would never become friends, irrespective of how much they bonded.

The only thought she could hope for was that she would get to work with the family again or work with someone like Riya's family.

*****

The next morning was a slow one, especially after the dancing continued well into the night from the Sangeet event. It was the day of the wedding, and the last pre-wedding ceremony was the ritual of applying turmeric to the bride and groom.

Since both families were staying at the same resort, the events were running in parallel. Seema checked on the groom's side of the event and was heading back to the bride's celebration when she heard a lot of shouting and laughing. She walked by one of the pools at the resort, wondering what the commotion was about, and that's when she saw Raghav being chased by a group of people. Every one of them, both men and women, had the yellow color stained on their face and hands, and it looked like they were chasing Raghav to apply the color to him.

She let out a laugh and plastered her back to the wall to get out of the way, but the moment Raghav spotted her, he stopped.

"Why is your phone turned off?" He was out of breath as he spoke, keeping an eye on the group who was relentlessly after him.

"You should run." She laughed.

"Where is your phone?" He stepped closer to her, and she looked at the group who got closer.

"Raghav—" Her words were lost in a squeal when he grabbed her by the shoulders, pulling her off the wall to make her stand in front of him like she was going to shield him from the group. "What are you doing?"

"Seema, get out of the way. It's time to get some color on his face and win that sweet prize money."

Raghav laughed. "Nice try, but sweet cousins and darling sister, I have a better deal for you."

"We don't care," one of the youngest cousins cried out.

"I will double the prize money that Dad declared only and only if you guys get Seema to put that yellow stuff on me."

"What?" Seema and the group said almost in unison.

"Deal or no deal?" Raghav rolled up his sleeves as if he had won already.

Riya thought for a moment. "Double, did you say?"

"Yes, you heard me right." He chuckled.

Riya grabbed a bowl of the turmeric mixture and said, "Seema, do this for me. Boys, hold him down."

Raghav shook his head. "No need to hold me. I'll stand like a statue if Seema is going to apply the color."

"Seema?"

Seema shook her head. "I... I can't—"

"Triple the amount if you convince her to start in under thirty seconds, or all bets are off."

Riya let out a growl. "Oh my God. Seema, take the bowl and do it."

"She is going to tell you guys that it's inappropriate for her to put color on me. I bet you."

"Seema, just do it," Riya encouraged.

Raghav smirked. "I dare you to, Ms. Seema Kumar."

How was he so sure she won't do it?

Seema held his gaze for a long moment and said, "Sure. Let's move over here so you can record this as proof to collect the prize."

"Good idea," the group murmured.

"Bring it on, Ms. Seema Kumar."

Seema picked up a big blob of the paste and smiled. "Patience, Mr. Vasudev."

"Seema, do it for the team. We get triple the prize money!" Riya cheered.

She rubbed the paste between her palms and took her hands to his face as she held his gaze, and his eyes darkened. She placed her paste-coated palms on his cheeks and heard his groan deep inside and watched as his eyes rolled shut.

A shudder passed through him, and it resonated deep inside her. She pulled her hands back, and his eyes flew open. "That doesn't count."

"Put more on him," the crowd cheered.

Seema took the paste and rubbed it evenly and whispered so only he heard, "I'll make this count."

Raghav was enjoying the playfulness and kept his eyes on her as she brought her hands to his cheeks again, and before he could relish her touch, she moved them down to his jawline, her thumbs running over his cheekbone.

The crowd cheered as she ran her fingers over his forehead, covering his face in the paste while he enjoyed his state of bliss. He was so lost in keeping his eyes locked with hers, he had not noticed she had slid her hands down his neck and had them firmly planted on his now heaving chest.

"This, Mr. Vasudev, is payback for pulling me into it."

Before he could realize what she meant, she pushed him, and the next thing he knew, his feet were unsteady as he walked backward, and then they were in the air as he fell into the pool behind him. He let out a grunt as his back hit the water, and he went under.

When he surfaced, he heard the laughter of his family, but his eyes searched for the woman who knew how to set him on fire.

He splashed the water on his cousins who were teasing him from the edge of the pool and let out a feral cry of joy.

"She is unbelievable," he groaned to himself as he pulled himself out of the pool, laughing.

Later that evening, Seema stood looking at herself in the mirror in awe of the beauty of the dress she had on. It was the same dress that changed many hands before it was gifted to her by Riya's grandmother.

"You look drop-dead gorgeous in that dress," Nandu said as she pinned her hair up for the wedding and reception that evening.

"Thank you. I love the color of the dress you are wearing. It makes you look so beautiful."

Nandu blushed. "Why, thank you. It was sweet of Riya's grandma to give us gifts."

"Yeah, that's very sweet. Let's go. Showtime." Seema followed Nandu as they left to check on Riya and Deepak before the ceremony started.

Seema walked toward the bridal suite and turned the corner. Her eyes met with those of the man she had been avoiding since yesterday. Her breath got stuck in her throat by the way his eyes widened as he spoke on the phone.

She looked away as she entered the bridal suite feeling some strange sensations. Raghav looked dapper in the semi-traditional outfit he had on, and there was no denying that the admiration she had for him had morphed into attraction. When, she didn't know.

"Seema, look at you. You look so beautiful."

"Thank you, Riya." Seema smiled and asked, "How are you feeling?"

"On top of the world. I can't wait to be Mrs. Deepak." She giggled.

"So happy to hear."

Riya leaned closer to Seema and planted a kiss on her cheek. "How can I thank you for getting Raghav to dance and this wonderful wedding. I asked for a unique wedding, and you have made it just so memorable."

Seema smiled. "You are a sweetheart, and we are so happy we were able to create these memories."

"I have so much to tell you but not now. When I get back from my honeymoon, I want you over at my place."

"Sure."

Riya hugged Seema and said, "Don't be a stranger. I consider you my good friend."

Riya's words melted Seema's heart, and she pulled back fighting emotions she had not felt before. She was overwhelmed by the strong feelings she was discovering for Raghav and the affection she was receiving from his family.

Enjoy the attention while it lasts. People are too busy to keep in touch with their wedding planner after the event.

Later that night, she was in the central control room running through the final checklist when her phone beeped a message.

Raghav: *Meet me by the pool in five?*

Seema: *How about in ten?*

Raghav: *Works.*

Seema walked toward the resort pool, where it was now quiet considering most of the guests had left soon after the bride and the groom left, and only a few family members hung out in the banquet hall.

She stopped when she saw Raghav stand by the pool, his back to her. She took a moment to observe him like she would not get to see him again after that night. She took in a soft, hissy breath realizing she was going to miss being around him and would be hungover him for a bit. He turned as if he felt her eyes on him and held her gaze as her heart kick-started in her chest.

Why did she have such a reaction every time?

She walked close to him. "You wanted to see me?"

"Yes, I would like to see you again after tonight. Can we meet for dinner this week?"

Her eyes widened in surprise to his direct question, but she smiled and said, "It is very nice of you to invite me for dinner, but—"

He interjected. "Seema, I can't stop thinking about you, and if I am not mistaken, you feel what I have been experiencing lately."

Her mouth went dry as he stepped closer to her. She kept her eyes locked with his as he gently placed his palm on her cheek. "I don't want to ignore what I feel for you."

"Raghav, it's not appropriate for us to—"

"Not anymore. We are two adults who have something brewing between them, and I'm saying we should not ignore it."

"What?" her voice was a whisper.

He leaned closer to plant a kiss on her cheek before taking her hand to his chest, where his heart thudded against her palm. "If you have a matching beat in your chest, come have dinner with me. I will send you details over a text."

She pulled her hand away from him and turned away, unable to handle the intensity of the moment.

What just happened? How did he get her heart to go on a rampage with a kiss on the cheek?

17

A few days later, Seema rolled in bed trying to avoid looking at the clock on her bedside table. She was on her break, just like her entire team that week, and she could continue to lay in bed, but she had a big dilemma to deal with.

The Bride's Brother. Why did he have to say those words that night?

He was the one making her mind go into overdrive while her heart tried to take charge of the situation.

"Seema, you still in bed?" Nandu laughed and added, "Are you going out with us?"

Seema smiled at Nandu standing at her bedroom door. "No. You guys go have fun."

"What's gotten into you this week? You are so lost."

Seema shrugged. "Nothing."

"Something is up. You've been awfully quiet the past few days."

Seema managed to smile. "I'm good. Have fun."

"See you later." Nandu left her to her thoughts and to the internal debate between her heart and mind that had been going on for a few days now—from the moment Raghav invited her to dinner and made his intentions clear.

Why did he have to do that? There was no denying that she had a strong infatuation toward him, but she would have gotten over him, eventually. Maybe, maybe not, but she knew it would have been painful just from the way she felt the past few days.

Her heart started to thud again when she remembered the way he looked at her. His eyes spoke volumes, the unspoken words her heart understood, and however much she tried to dismiss all her feelings as a deep attraction to how ideal of a man Raghav was, she could not. She finally looked at the clock, it was past five, and Raghav had said the reservations were for seven that evening.

"I want to go," she said out loud as if to silence the voice that had been putting more and more doubts in her mind.

She sat up and shook her shoulder as if to shake off the doubts she held and walked into the bathroom. The restaurant he had asked her to meet him at was a good thirty-minute ride from her apartment, and since she had been so distracted the past few days, she decided to take a cab to the restaurant.

She opened her closet and stood looking at her clothes. After a lot of back and forth, she settled for a baby-pink pleated skirt that hit below her knees and paired it with a black boatneck and cap-sleeved silk blouse. She chose the clothes she would be comfortable and cool in on the warm evening.

Forty-five minutes later, she waited for her cab to arrive. She was a nervous wreck and considered canceling a million times in the last ten minutes.

What is the problem? What could go wrong?

She closed her eyes, realizing that no matter where the dinner took them, she would be left heartbroken forever when things ended between them. They both were attracted to each other, and for her, there was no denying that she had not felt it deep inside. She didn't know when, but she had been falling in love with the idea of being with someone like him.

Don't you dare lie to yourself again. You want him, not just anyone like him.

She took in a hissy breath and fought back the pangs of anxiety as the cab rode through the slow traffic. She leaned her head back on the seat and wondered what the dinner meant for Raghav. A man who could have any woman he wanted told her he didn't want to ignore what he was feeling for her.

What if those feelings were temporary?

She closed her eyes unable to handle the crazy thoughts. She let the worst-case scenario play out in her head, and she knew she was about to shoot herself in the foot. There was still a chance to cancel, and she pulled out her phone to send him a text message.

As if he had somehow sensed her apprehension, she got a message from him.

Raghav: *Looking forward to seeing you.*

There was no going back. She was going to go through with this and knew she would end up hurting herself, but she could not get herself to deny what her heart wanted. It was easier to silence the inner voice a few days ago when he was still technically a client, but now, she had no way to contain her emotions that ran strong. Her pragmatic mind was slowly losing its battle with her heart and knew it was time to let go and listen to the thudding in her chest.

The cab pulled up in front of the building where the restaurant was on one of the top floors. She stepped out of the cab and took a deep breath before looking up the wide stairs that led into the lobby. As her eyes rose, they met those of the man who had been invading her thoughts and dreams for days.

Her breath got trapped when she saw him standing at the top of the steps as if he had been eager to see her. Her lips curved up inadvertently as he smiled at her. She went up the stairs, her eyes locked with his, and when she got closer, he placed one arm around her and brushed his lips over her temple.

Any residual apprehension that was left after she saw him was wiped away with the sweet kiss on her forehead.

"So good to see you," he whispered before leading her through the lobby, his hand gently caressing hers.

"Same here." She followed him to the bank of elevators and stepped into one of them as he held the door for her.

She walked to one corner of the elevator, and he walked to the other end, his eyes sparkling at her like he was overjoyed to see her. She smiled, the sparks in his eyes making her happy. Something about this man made her happy to the core as if she had no care in the world and no sadness could come near her.

"Someone looks happy." She held his gaze.

"That would be me because I've been miserable the past few days waiting to see you."

She looked away, unable to handle the moment of bliss as it felt like he had reached out and touched her. "I thought about you a lot as well."

"You did? Good."

His words made her blush, and she looked up when the elevator stopped and the doors opened. She let out a low gasp when she realized they had ridden up to the terrace of the building to the other section of the restaurant that was hard to get a table on any night.

He gently hooked his index finger into her little finger in the most adorable way as he led her through what seemed to be an empty restaurant.

"How come no one else is here?" she asked, curious the terrace garden restaurant was not bustling with guests, especially when the space was beautifully decorated with plants. Each table was a pod of greenery, and the privacy between tables was created by creepers and other plants.

A series of small bulbs illuminated each section while a large lamp hung from a plank-style roof, creating a cozy environment at each table.

"Tonight, it'll be just us." He stopped in the middle of the open space that was dimly lit with small bulbs and asked, "Where would you like to sit?"

She smiled as she looked around the space. "How is it that no one else is here?"

"I reserved the terrace for us, considering how much you like being surrounded by plants."

She let out a laugh looking around the beautiful space. "You managed to reserve the entire restaurant? How? It's so hard to get a table here."

He smirked. "Not hard when you own the place. Pick a table."

She looked at him, surprised, and something sparked in her mind. "Did Riya design this space?"

"Yes." He smiled.

"It's beautiful." She looked around the area taking in the peaceful space that looked beautiful on that breezy evening. The terrace had a service area to one side that was discrete, hidden behind large potted plants and a stage to one side high enough for everyone to see the performers.

"Amazing."

"Where do you want to sit?" He looked around the space, and Seema thought for a moment.

"I want to be where I can see the entire space, how about up there?" She pointed at the empty stage.

He chuckled. "You never cease to amaze me."

"What?" She let out a laugh.

He smiled as he pulled out his phone to type a few messages before looking at her. "Done."

"Seriously?"

"Yeah, we can hang out over there while our table is set up." He pointed to one side of the restaurant and gently touched her elbow as he walked to the other side of the open space.

"It's nice up here, and this is the perfect weather to be eating up here." She snuck a peek at him from the side, admiring his chiseled profile and was so lost in admiring him from up close, she didn't have the time to look away when he turned to look at her.

He held her gaze, smiling. "Glad you like it. What have you been up to?"

She shrugged, looking at the view of the city in the night lights. "On a break this week."

"What do you normally do on your breaks?" he asked.

"Normally, I just catch up on sleep, movies, and maybe some reading."

"What kind of movies do you watch?"

She kept her eyes on the city skyline. "I watch all kinds of movies, but the ones I like most are the classics."

"And you speak five languages, so you have a lot more options for movies." He chuckled.

She looked at him, taken aback. "How do you know that?"

He slowly turned to look at her. "How else would I know? You told me."

Her heart somersaulted that he took note of a detail only people she was close to knew. It was not a big deal for her to speak so many languages, but the fact he remembered amazed her.

"What do you do when you are free?" She was totally at ease as they continued their conversation, and she could not remember why she was so nervous to meet him.

"I spend most of my free time lazing on the couch catching up on sports or at the gym."

"And you cook, too."

"Not as much as I'd like to because I find it hard to find folks who are willing to be my guinea pigs."

"I thought it was sweet of you to cook for your family."

"But you didn't stay for lunch that day," he teased.

"Next time. I would like to be your guinea pig."

"Deal." He let out a laugh. "When? Can we set a date and time?"

She laughed, realizing he was, in a way, imitating her. "We just need to figure out when you have time."

"Anytime is a good time for me."

"I mean... you are so busy, I wasn't sure—"

"When will I get to see you again?" his tone shifted, and Seema looked up at him, a smile on her face that froze when her eyes met his, and her breath trapped in her throat.

Raghav was looking at her, his eyes holding an emotion she could not decipher. The moment felt powerful, and it made it feel like the ground under her feet shook in response.

He looked away when someone called out to him, and she realized she had been holding her breath. Her chest was heaving, and she didn't know how a casual conversation turned out to be heart-pounding.

"Let's go."

She smiled at him when he gently placed his palm on the small of her back and led her back to where a few people were setting up a table.

"This is so cool. I like this idea."

"Please," he said, pointing to the table that had two chairs set up on either side.

She looked at the setup and said, "I get dibs on that chair because it gives me a view, but I don't want you to face the wall."

He smirked. "Why would I be looking at the wall when you are in front of me?"

Seema bit her lip, suppressing the smile that would not go away and hoped he didn't notice how flushed her face was in the dim light. She sat down to eat, and very soon, they were lost in conversations about their childhood, his adventures as a prodigy and hers as a rebellious child who was moved from one orphanage to another, and how she crashed a wedding before she decided to become a wedding planner.

When the dessert was served, she looked at the plate and asked, "Is this what I think it is?"

He smirked. "What do you think it is?"

"No way." She looked at the familiar dish, the one they had shared when she was at his place for their dance practice.

"Yes, it is. In your own words, *your favorite dish.*"

"This is unbelievable." She dug her fork into the crusty dessert that was made out of dry fruits and nuts and had to have some magical potion as it tasted divine. She took a bite, and her eyes rolled shut in decadence as she let out a satisfied moan.

"I take it that it is still your favorite dish."

She opened her eyes and asked. "Did your mom make this?"

He nodded.

"What? For real?"

"I told my mom I was meeting someone for dinner, and she asked if it was the same woman who loved her dessert, and I said yes. The next thing I know, a delivery shows up with instructions that it is for my guest."

Seema blushed. "Oh, my God. This is so awesome and embarrassing at the same time."

"Why?"

"I mean... why did you put her through the trouble? You shouldn't have."

"It's no trouble. She is doing everything she can to help her son woo the woman he cannot stop thinking about."

His words hit her as a jolt of energy sliced through her, and her mouth went dry, not knowing what to say.

18

Seema's heart raced like a bullet train in her chest, and she lowered her eyes, unable to handle the rush of emotions.

"Seema, look at me." It was a plea.

She took a deep breath and raised her eyes to him slowly. "Raghav, let's not take this any further."

"Why?"

"It's... it's a bad idea."

"Why?" His tone was persistent.

She fell silent as her eyes lowered again, and a million reasons why there would be no future for them swarmed her mind.

Raghav got up from his chair to walk over to where she sat and kneeled in front of her. A few moments passed, and she kept her eyes lowered. He slowly moved his hand to gently touch her cheek before running his fingers under her chin to make her look at him.

"Seema..."

She raised her eyes to his, a lost expression in them. He cupped her cheek with his hand and said, "I... I can't breathe when you look at me like that."

"Raghav..." She let out a sob, unable to speak.

"Seema, there may be many reasons why this is a bad idea, but we need just one reason to give this a shot." He took her hand and flattened her palm on his chest. "This is not normal for me, and I can't ignore it. If you feel anything of what I am feeling, then that is the only thing we need not to give up on what we feel for each other."

She pressed her lips together and shook her head. "I want you, but—"

He silenced her, his lips gently brushing over her quivering ones before planting a kiss on her cheek. He lay a trail of kisses on her cheek before pulling back to look at her. "That is all I want to know, and everything else we can figure out. I have been waiting to hear those words. I want you, too, and I can't imagine being able to enjoy another moment without you. I want all your smiles, and I want those beautiful eyes to look at me and sparkle with joy. I want to be the one to fulfill every one of your dreams because you are my dream come true. I want—"

She wasn't listening anymore as she reached up and pressed her lips to his as her eyes closed. The moment was incredible. His lips were soft as she held on to him, one hand on his collar and the other around his neck. The sweetness at the moment, and the warmth and softness in his touch soothed the pain she never thought could be relieved. She felt at home.

She let out a moan when he pulled her closer, angling her head to deepen the kiss. His lips were cajoling as he robbed her of her breath. Her hand went up to his cheek, and she felt him groan in pleasure setting something off inside her.

When they both surfaced for air, he planted tender kisses on her cheeks and held her close to him with their foreheads touching. "Come home with me. Spend your break with me."

She smiled. "Are you sure you don't want a break from me?"

"I want you, all of you."

"What will I do at your place?"

"You can do whatever you want to. You can paint all the walls black or bring all the plants from outside into the house, eat all the desserts you want... anything. But I cannot be without you."

She smiled, knowing she would be lying to herself if she said she didn't feel the same way. "Raghav, I know what you mean, and I feel the same way, but what if... what if it doesn't last? You and I may be feeling this way because we've seen each other a lot the past few months."

He smiled, his lips running over hers as he pulled her closer. "We are not teenagers anymore."

She smiled, nodding. "So, what do you suggest we do?"

"Figure out what this is that we feel for each other." He stood up, pulling her with him, his arms tightly wrapped around her.

"And if... if it is..." Her words were lost when she looked into his eyes. The way he looked at her, she had no care in the world at that moment, and she knew not to question what they felt for each other.

She slowly went up on her toes to kiss him on his cheek, feeling him shudder in response to her touch. "I would like to spend my break with you."

He smiled gloriously. "Music to my ears. Let's go."

*****

Seema looked down at their clasped hands as they rode up the elevator to his apartment after stopping by her place and picking up some clothes. She had texted Nandu that she was taking a short trip and would return in a couple of days. It was a Thursday, and she was planning to head back Saturday morning.

She had no idea how she got herself to say yes to spending time with him when she was so apprehensive earlier that day about even meeting him. She leaned closer, hugging his arm, and liking the feel of his strong arms along her body.

"Are you sleepy?"

"No. I'm just thinking how I got myself to agree when I—" She stopped when the elevator doors opened.

"When you?" he prompted, carrying her overnight bag he refused to let her hold.

She hesitated to say it out loud because it pained her even to think what she would be doing if she hadn't left her apartment. She looked up at him as he held the door for her. "I even considered canceling after I got into the cab."

He leaned down to kiss her on the lips. "Don't worry, I would have shown up at your door if you didn't go tonight."

She smiled against his lips as he wrapped one arm around her waist, picking her feet off the ground like she weighed nothing and stepping indoors. "If you showed up, would you have kissed me like this?"

He groaned as he kicked the door closed with his foot and dropped her bag to the floor. He wrapped his other arm around her, his lips never leaving hers as he walked them to the large kitchen counter. His lips worshipped hers, and she wrapped her arms around his neck.

She let out a surprised grunt when she felt her bottom slide over the marble counter of the island in the kitchen. As if her response set off something in him, his lips turned eager, and his tongue slipped past her lips to tangle with hers in a hot dance. She was hot and out of breath by the time he let go of her mouth to slip his lips down her neck. She let out a moan of sheer pleasure.

She felt the gentle pull in her hair as he opened up her neck for the seductive invasion. She hugged his head and arched her back, one hand landing flat on her palm on the counter as his lips trailed along the 'V' of her silk blouse.

She felt the heat from his breath ignite something deep inside, and she threw her head back invitingly as he kissed every inch of her exposed skin, his arm supporting her back while the other hand ran over her bottom, keeping her close to him.

The spark that he set off inside her only grew with every kiss. She wanted more of him and wanted to hold and kiss him. With her growing need, she pushed into him, her hand coming off the counter as she leaned into him.

"Raghav," her voice was hoarse as she found his hungry lips.

"Baby, this is not what I planned for tonight."

"Me neither." She breathed into his neck, eager for his taste. She grazed her teeth over the throbbing in his neck and felt a shiver pass through him.

He let out a groan when she sucked in the skin on his neck between her teeth. "You're going to turn me into a caveman if you keep doing that, and that'll scare you away."

She smiled, kissing along his neck and then on the deep dent on his chin before pulling back and looking into his eyes that were deep with desire. "Maybe that's my getaway plan."

He chuckled, pulling her closer. "I'm not going to let you get away so quickly."

She smiled, happy to be in his arms. "What do you want to do now?"

"Whatever you want to do."

"Really? You want me to stay that badly?"

He kissed her cheek, making her smile before stepping away from her to go to the refrigerator. "I thought I made that pretty clear. What would you like to drink?"

"Can I get a soda, and we can go watch the oldest movie you have in your collection?" Her eyes followed him while she remained on the kitchen counter.

"Done."

A few hours later, Seema moved in her sleep and let out a moan enjoying the feel of the warmth that swarmed her.

"Raghav." His name rolled off her lips inadvertently, and she felt his lips sweep over her temple. That's when she realized he was holding her, and she opened her eyes, aware of the fact that he had carried and laid her on the bed. The last thing she remembered was watching a classic Italian movie and her eyes straining to read the subtitles.

"Good night," he said, smiling, and was about to walk away when she held his hand.

"Sleep here. The bed is big enough for both of us."

He looked around and chuckled. "I probably should. I've never slept in the guest bedroom." She blushed when he leaned closer and kissed the back of her hand that held his. "I'll be back in a minute."

He left the room, and she suddenly felt a cold draft sweep over her. She pulled the sheets over her body as a new unsettling feeling started to grow.

Where was she and what was she doing there?

The room suddenly made her feel like she was an alien amidst the luxury and style the space exuded. She felts pangs of anxiety grip her, and her breath started to hiss.

Big mistake. Get out while you can. You don't fit in his world.

That was it, the reason for her apprehension. It wasn't that his family was a client at some point but the fact that their worlds were entirely different. He had a rich heritage in the form of family lineage, and she was a nobody and would be that way forever.

She snapped out of her thoughts that she didn't know how long she had been reeling in, but he knew immediately that something was off. "Seema, what's wrong?"

Her breath was hissy as he came to her side and pulled her to him, her cheek hitting his chest. "I... I don't belong."

"What?" He pulled back to look at her as her body trembled.

"Raghav, we are worlds apart. I don't belong here."

"You. Belong. Here." He pointed to his chest before he pulled her into his arms. The warmth from his embrace and the comfort from his touch wiped out all of her worries as she slipped into a deep slumber.

19

Seema still had her eyes closed as she surfaced from a deep sleep. It took her a moment to remember that she was on a break and could sleep longer. She moved in her sleep, and the warmth and coziness that wrapped around her made her smile, reminding her of the man who had managed to steal the last bit of her heart when he hugged her as they fell asleep in each other's arms.

His chest was plastered to her back, and his arm fell loosely around her waist as she rested her head on his forearm. She smiled as she moved to kiss the arm she lay on before rolling around slowly to face him.

She observed him as he slept, and instead of kissing him and running the risk of waking him up, she kissed his upper arm, a sweet smile on her lips. She wanted him, to be with him, and everything made sense.

Was it that simple?

She snuggled closer, gently kissed his arm, and slowly raised her eyes to find him looking at her. She blushed when their eyes met, and she buried her face in his chest. He planted a kiss on the top of her head and said, "Good morning."

She gently pulled away to look at him for a long moment before kissing him on her favorite spot, the sexy cleft on his chin hidden behind his stubble. "Good morning."

"Will you stop teasing me like that?"

"What?" She let out a laugh.

He pulled her close to him, his lips barely a thread from hers, and said, "If you are going to kiss me, then do it right, don't tease me."

She smiled, holding the space between them and sticking her tongue out to trace his lower lip as his eyes rolled shut. He opened them, and the look in his eyes sent waves of thrill to the apex of her legs, making her quiver.

He groaned like he was in deep pain. "Seema, cut it out."

"I don't know any other way to kiss," she whispered, sucking his lower lip between her teeth.

He dug his fingers into her flesh, making her breath hiss. "You and I will never get out of bed if you keep up with this."

She smiled coyly as she pulled back. "Maybe I should stop kissing you, then."

He chuckled, running his fingers through her hair, pulling her into a hard kiss before letting go of her mouth. "That's how you kiss, and I will show you more variations once I get you some coffee."

"I would love to get that kissing lesson." She laughed, watching him walk away as her heart pounded for him, and she knew it would, forever.

Later that morning after she had showered, she wandered out of the guest bedroom and into the home office, curious about the shields and mementos on the wall. She got closer to them reading the wordings on the awards wondering if they were similar to what she had seen at his parents' house.

She let out a laugh when she read the words on one of the mementos.

Vasudev Rayala Family Reunion – Sports and Games Champion

Seema looked around the room and saw he had many such awards for various games, and it looked like Raghav had won a lot of them. She smiled when she realized he had kept his family- related accomplishments with him and his professional mementos at his parents' place.

"I see you found the Wall of Fame." He chuckled, walking up to kiss her on her bare shoulder, making her head drop to his chest.

"I am so impressed with your accomplishments."

He let out a laugh. "These are the ones I'm most proud of."

She turned around, smiling at him. "Explains why your cousins were trying to win by putting the turmeric on you."

"And I got my favorite woman to put that paste on me."

She let out a laugh. "For triple the prize money."

"Totally worth it." He winked before pulling her into a deep kiss.

She pulled back, a challenge in her eyes. "You need to play with me and win."

"Yeah? Which game?"

She narrowed her eyes at him. "Any game."

"You just challenged the defending champion of the family tournaments."

"Oh, I'm scared." She wiggled her shoulders feigning fear.

A few hours later and four different games played, she kept her focus on the red coin on the board as they played carrom pool, and Raghav was on the verge of losing the fourth game in a row.

"How the frack is this possible?"

She hushed him without looking up, but she knew he was royally pissed. "You sound like a sore loser."

He fell silent as she finished the strikes and let out a squeal of joy. "Now, Mr. Vasudev, that's how you win tournaments."

"Beginners' luck. Let's pick another game." He stormed into his study, and she followed, laughing.

"Raghav, it's so adorable to see you like this."

"Right." He snickered.

She stepped in front of him between his broad chest and the bookshelf he had opened and wrapped her arms around him. "I would like my kissing classes now. No more board games."

"Not cool." He looked into her eyes, unamused.

"I have been thinking about how I should be really kissing, and I think I know now. Can I try?"

His eyes clouded with a deep longing, but his facial expression didn't change. She smiled as she went up on her knees, and as if to rub in the tease, she nipped on his chin, making him growl. Her smile widened as she moved her lips to his cheek and then laid a trail of butterfly kisses along his jawline, her breath starting to hiss.

What had started as a playful way of distracting him had turned into something powerful, something that both of them felt deep inside and knew they could not contain anymore. He moved his hands to run over her back, pulling her close to him, and she felt his hard desire against her belly.

She wrapped her arms around him, and he clashed their lips together denting her stomach with his hardness as she rolled her hips as if to stroke him. He groaned against her lips as if he lost all resolve when she started matching his fervor of the kiss.

"Baby, I can't wait. I want you." His confession made a ripple of pleasure shred through her, making her squirm with unhandled need.

"I... I want you, too." She used her arms as anchors to hug his neck and hoisted herself, wrapping her legs around him.

He kissed her, and she let out a cry of joy as he carried her out of the study toward his bedroom. She clung to him while taking in the moment, where they were about to share something special she knew would be etched in her heart and mind forever.

She had been in his bedroom when he had given her the tour of his place, but that same room suddenly felt like it was their space, like she shared it with Raghav.

How is that even possible?

She brushed away the last of the questions as he lowered her onto the bed, her back hitting the mattress before he rolled her onto him, his lips finding the crook of her neck. He nipped on the delicate skin making her throb deep inside.

She called out his name as an unhandled surge of emotion coursed through her, and a need to be with him, filled by him, surmounted. She sat up, pulling away from his mouth, straddling him as he lay on the bed, their eyes doing all the talking.

His hands reached for the hem of her t-shirt, and he pulled it off over her head in a flash. She blushed by the way he looked at her bra-clad chest as he ran his hands up her torso. He then pulled her onto him to trailed kisses on her chest along the hem of the bra cup, making her moan.

She ran her fingers into his thick dark hair as she tried to catch her breath. Her heart was beating so rapidly to his slow seduction, she was slick and ready for him. She let out a cry of pleasure when he pushed aside the fabric covering her breasts with his teeth before his mouth closed around her pebbled nipples. She had a tornado of pleasure building as he kissed, sucked, and nibbled on every inch of her skin, and she knew she needed him deeper inside to satiate her growing need.

"Raghav... I..." She could only gasp.

"Baby, you are so hot right now, you are driving me nuts." He let go of her flesh from his hot mouth before pushing her back onto the mattress, his weight delectably pinning her down as he reached for something in the drawer of the nightstand.

She was quick to take off his t-shirt to run her palms over his chiseled torso while he went for her loose-fitting pants, pulling them down with her panties. She gasped in response to the feral look in his eyes and watched in utter fascination as he went down to run his tongue over the throbbing between her legs.

Goosebumps peppered her skin as he closed his lips over the apex of her thighs, his tongue engaging with her drenched folds. She held his head with one hand while she clung to the pillow with the other, burying her face into the softness.

She moaned, unable to handle the wave of emotions and sensations she had never felt before. She raised her hips off the mattress as if she could not get enough of the feel of his mouth on her. The wave was now an uncontrollable tsunami of thrills, and she held her breath to brace herself for the landfall. When it did, she came undone and was still shuddering from the pleasure when he came up to kiss her, making her moan into his mouth.

He held her to him, running his hot rod over her clenched folds and engaged their mouths as he entered her, making her complete. She hugged him as he built a rhythm while riding the wave of emotions that gave her heart the calm she had been looking for, for years.

He was the one for her, and there was no one else who could have her heart. He owned her entirety—mind, body, and soul—and she loved him with everything she had.

"I love you, Raghav." The words rolled off her lips, barely a whisper, and they both peaked together. He groaned into her neck as he collapsed onto her before pulling her to him as he rolled on his side.

His heart pounded against her cheek as she drifted into a deep state of bliss and to the last of his words playing in her ear. "I will love you forever."

20

Seema looked at herself in the mirror as she adjusted her hair and had decided to skip the high-pony look. She was nervous as she ran her hands down the long dress she had chosen to wear to Raghav's parents' house.

It had been two weeks since the time she and Raghav got together, and she had never been so happy in her life. She had started working on another wedding project that was scheduled six months out, and Nandu was focusing on the surprise anniversary events. She was out of town rallying with Mr. Rayudu at his native place, so she could scope the space without letting out the details of the event.

She looked at her phone when she saw it was ringing. Raghav was calling. She smiled as she answered the call but stayed silent.

"Baby, you still can't be angry with me. I wanted you to be there with my family." Raghav chuckled.

A week back, Raghav had invited her to attend the family dinner his parents were hosting since Riya and her new husband were back from their honeymoon, but she had declined saying it was too soon. But being the persistent guy he was, he had figured out a way for her to join the family. She could not say no when Riya had called to invite her and Nandu. She agreed to attend since Nandu was on the trip with the Janata Seva Party.

"C'mon, baby. Please don't be mad. I promise to let you eat all the dessert tonight."

She bit her lip, suppressing the smile. "I'm almost ready to go."

"I'm here. Don't forget to bring your bag. I missed you like crazy this past week."

He had been away on a business trip for the past week, and she could not wait to be with him. "I missed you, too."

Seema gathered her belongings along with the overnight bag she had packed to spend the weekend at Raghav's place. She was yet to share her relationship status with Nandu as she wasn't ready yet. She was sure she loved him and could not imagine not being with him, but something kept nagging her about the future.

Until she had the assurance deep inside that what she and Raghav shared would mature and last and not burn out in a few weeks, she was not ready to share with anyone. She was glad Raghav was respectful of her wishes to keep their relationship under wraps.

Seema stepped out of the elevator to find Raghav waiting for her. There were a lot of families and children gathered on the lowest level, and she smiled at her neighbors as she walked toward him. He reached for the bag in her hands before planting a kiss on her forehead, making the familiar thrill pass through her like every time he brushed his lips on her temple.

"I missed you so much," he whispered before stepping back to open the door for her.

Her breath hissed in response to the depth in his voice, but she could not find the words to reciprocate. She had no idea what she would do if things didn't work out between them, and however much she tried not to think about it, she couldn't.

"You okay?" he asked as she sat silently.

She smiled, looking in his direction before leaning to her side to kiss him on his cheek. "I'm good. I'm nervous."

He pulled her back into a kiss when she was about to move her lips away from him and said, "You are there to meet Riya and listen to every one of her honeymoon adventures."

She smiled, knowing how detailed Riya explained everything, especially when it was something she loved so much. "I can't wait to see Riya."

"She has been talking nonstop about her adventures in Africa, and the fact that I was in Malaysia all week didn't matter to her." He chuckled.

"I can't wait to hear all about her trip."

"You are in for a treat, then." He let out a laugh as he drove through the city traffic on Friday evening.

"What are we doing this weekend?" she asked, looking forward to being with him. She had met him a couple of times for lunch before he left for his Malaysia business trip and could not wait for alone time with him.

"We are going out tomorrow evening."

She turned to look at him. "Where are we going?"

"It's a surprise." He winked, looking at her for a brief moment before looking at the road.

"You like giving surprises now?" She let out a laugh.

"Why not? The woman I love tells me I should do more of that," he teased, making her blush.

"What are we doing on Sunday, then?"

"Whatever you want to do."

"Maybe we pick up where we left off with the board games."

"Yeah? Someone is getting used to winning. Is that why?"

"No. That's not it."

"Really? It's not about winning?" he scoffed.

"I... I love playing with you."

"Because I lose every time, and you get a kick out of the win?"

She fell silent, and he knew something was off. He placed his hand on her leg for a brief moment and said, "We can play tomorrow and on Sunday, baby."

She nodded, smiling and said, "As a kid, I loved playing all the board games, but—"

A lump formed in her throat, and her words were lost in a sob that she managed to suppress. "You'll know when we play tomorrow."

"Sure. And we are—" His phone started to ring on the car Bluetooth speakers, and she smiled when she saw it was Riya calling.

"Riya, why are you calling me so many times?" Raghav teased.

"I want to make sure you don't forget that you are supposed to pick up Seema on your way here."

"Yes, ma'am. Your precious package has been picked up and is in transit."

"Awesome! I can't wait to tell Seema everything."

"I'm sure she is excited to hear everything. Remember, you have already told me everything, so spare me the details."

"Whatever. I'll see you soon."

Riya ended the call, and Raghav let out a scoff. "She is such a child."

Seema shook her head. "She is a grown woman, married now, runs a successful business, and I'm sure she is still the baby of the house."

"This is true. She will hold the baby status until she has a baby."

She laughed. "Or until you have one."

"That's right. Just let me know when you are ready, and we can work on that, so Riya is not treated like a baby anymore." He chuckled.

Seema's breath hitched, and she didn't know what to say or how to react but managed to smile. "Stop joking, Raghav."

"Who said I'm kidding." He kept his eyes on the road as he pulled off the main road to the side street that led to his parents' house. Seema stayed silent while she tried to even out her breathing and was surprised by how much the idea appealed to her.

Being the mother of Raghav's child.

Too good to be true.

The undying voice still surfaced from time to time, and it sent a shiver through her as if in warning. She shook away the gloom that was settling in when he pulled the car up in front of the house. "I'll go mingle with the guests and come find you, baby."

"I'll be fine." She stepped out of the car as Raghav handed the car keys to one of the attendants and walked toward the front yard, where a group was gathered, while she headed into the house that was lit up beautifully for the occasion.

"Seema," she heard Riya call out to her from the front yard and smiled, waiting for the newlywed as she speed-walked toward her.

"Riya, you are glowing." Seema smiled as Riya hugged her.

Riya blushed. "I'm glowing because I just got back from my honeymoon, but what's the secret behind your glow?"

Seema stuttered not knowing what to say, but happy Riya came up with her theory. "I'm sure the stress of not having to deal with me every minute gave you the glow."

Seema shook her head. "It was my pleasure working with you."

"So glad you still think that way. I have an idea that I want to talk to you about but not tonight. I want you to enjoy yourself tonight."

Seema nodded. "Thank you so much for inviting Nandu and me for dinner tonight. Unfortunately, Nandu could not join as she is out of town."

"All good. And before I get pulled into another conversation, I need to show you the articles in the bridal magazines." Riya sounded excited.

"I can't wait."

"Let's go look at them. They are in the office." Riya led Seema through the beautifully decorated hallway to the home office where Seema and Riya had met months ago.

Riya opened the door and let out a surprised squeal. "Oh, Nani, you made the escape already?"

Riya's grandmother smiled and hushed her. "It's too noisy out there. I prefer being here."

"You are such a spoiled sport, Nani," she said and looked at Seema. "You remember Seema?"

"Yes, of course. Good to see you, Seema. You look lovely in that dress." The elderly woman put away her book.

"Good to see you, too. Sorry if we are disturbing you." Seema smiled.

"Not at all, dear. I just don't like it when people get too loud. Feel free to come find me here when you are sick of talking to everyone."

"Nani, Seema is here to have fun. Don't ruin the party for her."

Riya flipped through the magazines, her eyes sparkling at the pictures that were posted. Seema was thrilled to see the name of her company noted in the articles. She spent a little bit more time with Riya looking through the magazines and was happy that her team was able to exceed Riya's expectations.

Seema and Riya got up to leave and said their goodbyes to the older woman who continued reading her book. The elderly woman winked at Seema. "You know where to go if it gets too loud out there."

A short while later, she was in the middle of a conversation with some of Riya's friends when she felt his presence.

"Hello, ladies. Would you mind if I stole Ms. Seema Kumar for a bit?"

The women smiled awkwardly as they walked away from the group. "Raghav, that was so weird. Don't do that."

"Okay, I won't. Now walk with me." He led her toward the back of the house and to what looked like a service elevator.

"Where are you taking me?"

"You'll see." He planted a kiss on her lips as the elevator doors closed and added, "I missed you all evening. I can't keep up with this secret. I want to tell everyone."

Seema smiled. "Soon. I want to be the one to tell the people I care about."

"Fine. Let's go." He led her out of the elevator as she wondered what floor of the house they were on as they walked through the dimly lit space.

"Where are we going?"

He didn't respond immediately but waited for them to step into one of the rooms and shut the door before turning on the light. "All right, your turn to pick the game. And I need to figure out how not to lose, badly."

She let out a laugh, covering her mouth with her hand as she looked at the wall-to-wall shelf stacked with boxes of board games, some multiple editions arranged neatly. "This is amazing. I've never seen so many board games."

"Okay, pick your game to play with me."

Seema smiled and reached for him to put her arms around him, her heart thumping in her chest. "I love you, Raghav."

"Baby, look at me."

Seema pulled back to look at him. "Raghav... I..."

Raghav kissed her on her cheek. "Seema, you are the best thing that has happened to me, and I would lose any game, anything for that matter, any number of times, to have you in my life."

Seema let out a sob. "Growing up, I never had anyone to play with me. I was all by myself when I played the games at the orphanage, and I played both players. I don't care for the game we are playing, but all I want is to play with you. Will you play board games with me, forever?"

His eyes lit up as he smiled gloriously. "I would love that, and hopefully soon, I will learn to beat you at the games."

"Raghav, I want to be yours."

"You are all mine, love."

21

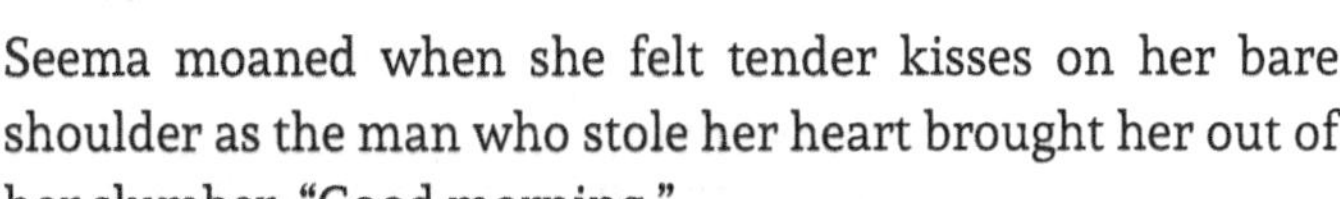

Seema moaned when she felt tender kisses on her bare shoulder as the man who stole her heart brought her out of her slumber. "Good morning."

"Good morning," she said, turning to face him.

His eyes fell on the bright red telling mark on her neck, and he ran his thumb over it. "Sorry, I hurt you. I got carried away."

She smiled, taking his thumb between her teeth and biting down gently. She saw how his eyes clouded and said, "I liked it."

He kissed her on her lips before sliding his hand over the length of her neck. "We have to go. We have a few hours of drive."

"Why are you being so secretive?" She hugged him.

"You'll see why."

"Okay. I will need thirty minutes, and I will be ready to go." She pulled her robe around her as she got out of bed.

"Does that include a shower with me?" He pulled her back on to the bed.

"No." She laughed and added, "Then I would need more than thirty minutes, don't you think?"

He kissed the top of her head. "I need every minute of my life to be with you."

His words sent a warning wave through her, and she buried her face into his chest, unable to silence the worry that would not quit.

"Seema, what are you not telling me?"

She let out a sob and decided it was time to share everything with him, even her worst thoughts. "I'm scared, Raghav."

"Why, love?"

"What if something happens, and I can't be without you?"

"What are you talking about?"

She took a deep breath. "The last time I trusted someone to be a life partner, I was left heartbroken because I was a nobody, and that fact has not changed even now, and—"

He silenced her with a kiss swallowing her sob and with it her doubts. He pulled back to look at her, her face cradled in his hands as he wiped away the moisture on her cheeks. "Seema, I fell for the woman in front of me, for the person she is, the caring heart, and that brain of yours that blows my mind. I love you for who you are and not what your parents or others have done."

"What if we never find out who I really am?"

"It doesn't matter. I only care about the woman who rules my heart. What she wants and her happiness will be of my utmost importance."

"What if—"

"My family?" he prompted.

She nodded. "They may be okay with me being an acquaintance but not someone you are with, what if they say we..."

She couldn't even get herself to finish the thought.

"Sweetheart, don't worry."

Seema pulled back to look at him. "Promise me that you will choose family if you have to choose between your people and me."

"Everything that's yours is mine, and all of me is yours. Ours." His voice was soft yet stern.

"I don't worry about anything when I'm with you, but when I'm not, I worry something will go wrong."

He pulled her to him, her cheek to his heart. "I'm right here for you."

She hugged him, feeling the weight from the worry lift, and wrapped her arms around him, never wanting to let go.

A short while later.

"We have been on the road for over an hour. How much longer?"

Seema was dying with the suspense of where he was taking her.

"Maybe twenty more minutes." He smiled, his eyes hidden behind aviator sunglasses that made him look stunning and sexy.

She looked back at her phone and looked at the map again. "Twenty more minutes and at this speed, it should be within thirty miles."

"Will you give that detective brain of yours a rest?"

"I need to know, and you told me you'll let me cook dinner for you if I can guess."

He chuckled. "First, you beat me at the board games, and now you are trying to steal my last job I have left in the house?"

"You cook for me all the time." She pouted.

"If you are okay with everyone knowing about us, then I can ask the staff to come back, so we can eat good food, and I get to spend all my time with you," he teased.

She thought for a moment. "Maybe we should tell everyone. Why don't we start with Nandu and Riya?"

"I like that. I like that very much."

She ran her hand along his thigh, playfully. "So, where are we going now?"

He laughed. "Nice, try. Sit tight until we get there."

"Whatever," she said, looking out the window. She saw something that caught her eye, and when she realized where he could be taking her, she was overwhelmed with joy. "Raghav, are you taking me to your ancestral home?"

He smiled. "Yes."

She let out a squeal of joy. "Oh my God. This is surreal. I get to see the inside, too?"

"The whole tour from your personal guide."

She unclicked her seat belt and hugged him. "I love you."

He kissed her, pushing her back to her seat and clipping her seat belt back on, laughing. "You can sit on my lap all night long."

"Raghav, I cannot believe this. I get to see the beautiful house and hear all that history. I love it."

From the time she had seen the family portrait in front of the beautiful historic building that was more like a palace, she had wanted to go there and know more about the history. She was beyond thrilled that Raghav knew what her heart longed for. She wanted him, and with the last speck of doubt about the future, it vanished into thin air like it never existed.

She knew she could handle anything with Raghav by her side, and she would give her everything for his happiness.

Seema looked out the window as the car moved through small villages with people going about their business even on a weekend. It was as if she were suddenly transported to another world. "I've never been to a village."

He chuckled. "I never expected the Ms. Poised Seema Kumar to have this side."

She laughed, enjoying the feel of the earthy air in her hair. "I didn't know I had this side, either."

"I can't imagine how you will be when you get in touch with your family."

She shook her head. "This would be nothing. If I found a family member, even a distant relative, I would be standing on top of a car on my way to meet them."

"I hope to witness that soon."

"Me, too," she said, suddenly hopeful about finding her own roots.

A short while later, he drove off the small road onto what looked like a private driveway. The shrubbery was overgrown on the sides, the tree branches casting a shadow as they drove on the mud road. He stopped when they came up to fenced gates.

"Is this it?" she asked as she saw the man at the guard post approach Raghav's side.

She watched as Raghav spoke to the man giving him instructions for their lunch, dinner, and snacks and drove through the tall gates.

"How long have you been planning this trip?"

"Not long, but the moment I thought of it, I knew you would like it." He smiled.

"How long are we staying here?"

He shrugged. "We can leave whenever you want."

"If it were up to me, I might want to stay the entire weekend." She laughed.

"I can see that."

Later that evening, after touring the antique house and then the surrounding fields on a bicycle, they both settled in for dinner. The family who lived on the premises was working on their dinner while they both sat on the terrace, sipping on their drinks by a concrete fire pit.

"Raghav, it is so beautiful, I could spend all night here." She leaned into him, hugging his arm.

He pulled her to him, kissing the top of her head. "We could."

She pulled back to look at him. "For real?"

He shrugged. "As long as you say yes to what I am about to ask you."

"I'll do anything." She stood up, looking around the space.

He reached for something in his pocket and pulled himself up to kneel in front of her. He opened the small box to reveal an antique ring. "Will you marry me, Ms. Seema Kumar, and be my wife?"

Her mouth went dry, and she froze. When he said she had to say yes, the question he asked was the last thing she expected.

"Seema. I promise to love you forever. Marry me."

"Yes, yes, yes." She kneeled as he slipped the ring on her finger and pulled her into a devouring kiss.

Happy tears rolled down her eyes as he kissed her cheeks. "You made me a very happy man today, sweetheart."

"I still can't believe it." She stared at the ring on her finger. "Is this a family heirloom?"

"Welcome to the family."

Seema let out a sigh. "I never thought I would see this day. Am I dreaming?"

Raghav laughed, shaking his head. "You are my dream come true. I don't want to spend another minute of my life without you. Move in with me."

She let out a laugh and nodded, unable to speak. Seema never expected a day like this would be a part of her life, her story. "We are engaged. We should tell everyone."

He pulled her to him, rolling her back onto the blankets, kissing her in the crook of her neck. "You can tell the whole world tomorrow, but tonight you are all mine."

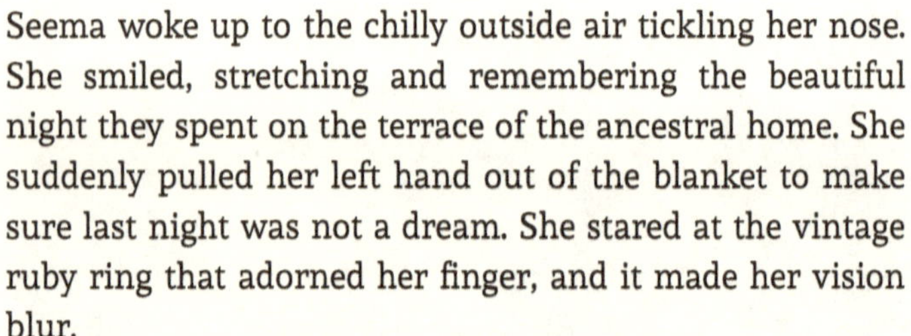

Seema woke up to the chilly outside air tickling her nose. She smiled, stretching and remembering the beautiful night they spent on the terrace of the ancestral home. She suddenly pulled her left hand out of the blanket to make sure last night was not a dream. She stared at the vintage ruby ring that adorned her finger, and it made her vision blur.

The ring was like no other she had seen in all the years she had been planning weddings. The three rubies that were on the ring would be categorized as mismatched color by a jeweler, the gold would have been deemed as scratched by an assessor, but for her, the history and the symbol of love the ring served as, made it priceless. It was perfect.

She slowly turned to look at the man who turned everything about her life to beautiful in such a short amount of time. She bent down to gently kiss him without waking him up before grabbing her phone to call Nandu to tell her everything.

It was still early on a Sunday morning, but she knew her best friend would not mind being shaken awake to hear the news about her engagement. She heard Nandu's voice after barely a ring.

"You are up early, too?" Nandu laughed.

"Yeah, how is the rally going?"

Nandu let out a sigh. "This is a lot of work, and we need to plan ahead, Seema. And these brothers are workaholics like you."

Seema laughed. "Then you don't miss me at all."

"Not a bit and guess what, the Rayudu's family home here is a beautiful location for—" Nandu's voice was lost when a rooster crowed in the background. "Seema, where the heck are you? Did you bring us a pet rooster?"

"No." She laughed and saw Raghav had woken up to the rooster's call and was shooing it away. "I'm out for the weekend."

"Out? Where?"

"I'm at Raghav's ancestral home?"

"What are you doing there? Checking it out for an event?" Nandu asked innocently, making Seema feel guilty.

"I... I've kept something from you for a while now, and I didn't tell you only because I didn't know where this would go, and—"

Nandu interjected, letting out a squeal of joy. "Who is the guy? Someone I know?"

"Yes, you do know him." She blushed, looking at Raghav who had fallen asleep with the sheets pulled over his head.

"Oh my God. Is it Brozilla?"

Seema let out a laugh. "Brozilla is also your best friend's fiancé now."

"Shut the front door. You are kidding me," Nandu was screaming into the phone. "The one weekend I am out of town, and all this happens? Unbelievable."

"I'm still processing everything."

Nandu laughed. "I should have known by the way he was looking at you. I told you he wasn't looking at you to ensure the quality of the tasks. That was the look. I knew it, and we have a lot to talk about."

"I'll see you tomorrow at work." Seema smiled to herself.

"No. I'll be home tonight," Nandu said and immediately started laughing. "Oh, right. You are saying you are not coming home?"

"Yes, Nandu, and we also need to talk because he asked me to move in with him, but I didn't want to say anything without asking you."

"You are mad, my friend. If you have agreed to marry him, you love him, and why would you be anywhere else?"

Seema let out a sigh. "Let's talk tomorrow."

"Yes, ma'am."

*****

"Why do you look so nervous?" Raghav asked later that evening after returning from his grandfather's village. "I just told my mom and dad, and they are ecstatic."

Seema smiled. "I think I should tell Riya."

"Really?" he teased.

"I don't know, you should call her." She shook her head with confusion.

Raghav thought for a moment. "I have an idea. Why don't we video call her? That way you get to tell her, too."

Seema nodded, but something was not sitting well. "We should have shared the news in person with friends and family. Riya is such a firm believer in face-to-face communication. I feel like we should tell her in person."

"You've studied her way too well." He laughed.

Seema blushed. "She has been so kind to me. Even though you are the brother, I want to be the one to tell her."

Raghav shrugged and put his phone away. "I told my parents not to tell her, and we can meet her for lunch or dinner tomorrow and tell her."

Seema nodded. "I think—"

Raghav let out a laugh when he saw his sister was video calling him. "Speak of the devil."

"Riya, what's happening?" Raghav held the phone in such a way she could see only him on the screen.

"I don't know, brother. I just happened to stop by Mom's, and they are all bursting with excitement, and I can't squeeze a drop out of them. What did you do?" Seema laughed.

"What do you think?"

"Based on their expressions, you told them the mystery woman is the one you want to be with."

Raghav chuckled. "Really? You don't think any of my professional accomplishments would make them so happy?"

"Did you get another award? Another 30 under 30 award?" She laughed and added, "I doubt it. No award or reward will make them bounce off the walls like this. It's got to be very personal."

"I'm impressed, little sis."

She nodded, rubbing her chin. "Based on Nani's expression, I get the feeling you have the family engagement ring out of the box."

"Riya Deepak Holmes. You are on to something." Raghav laughed.

Riya let out a squeal of joy, enjoying her accomplishment of being able to guess the reason. "Oh my God, I can't believe it. I am so happy for you. Who is she? Do I know her?"

"C'mon, I know how much you love playing these guessing games. You got this," he encouraged, looking at Seema who had been blushing all along, her heart overflowing with love for him.

How did she get so lucky?

"Yes. Wait. I need to remember. Oh, is it the woman you shared the dessert Mom made? The one who liked my wall at your place?"

"I like the way you think, Riya. Yes, that's her."

"So, you've been dating her since then?"

He shook his head. "Let's just say I was single even three days after your wedding."

"Wow, you fell in love in three weeks?" Riya gasped.

Raghav slowly looked at Seema who had her eyes on him. "I think I had fallen for her a while back and just didn't know it. I knew she was the one, the night of the Sangeet."

"This is uncanny. Remember when I told you I liked this guy, who is now my sweet husband? That was at my best friend's Sangeet."

"Yes. I remember." He smirked.

"I have never seen you like this. You are so in love."

Raghav looked at Seema. "I love her."

Riya let out an endearment. "That is so sweet. I'm so happy you found love."

Raghav kept his eyes on Seema. "Yeah, I knew it was her, but she is such a toughie. She made me work for her love."

Seema blushed, looking away from him.

"Raghav, she is there with you, isn't she? Please? Can I say hi?" Riya pleaded.

"Riya, you know the rules of the game."

"Fine. Fine. Give me something else. Another clue."

Raghav looked at Seema for a long moment. "All I can tell you is the woman I love has a beautiful heart, caring as hell, and only knows how to give but has never taken anything in return. I want to give her everything she ever wished for and more."

"Don't make me cry now. I had no idea you were such a stupid romantic." Riya let out a laugh as she wiped the moisture from the edge of her eyes.

"I didn't know either until I met her, and the first time I couldn't care less for her, but now, she rules my friggin heart." He locked his eyes with Seema's, making her heart somersault in her chest.

"Seema! Are you in love with Seema? It has to be her." Riya let out a cry of joy.

"You have gotten really good at this, little sis."

"Oh my God. It is Seema." There was a loud scream of joy and the sound of the phone being dropped on the floor before Riya came back. "I am so happy for you. I want to hug you two, kiss you. I want you guys to have a dozen babies and be happy forever."

Raghav laughed. "Thank you, Riya."

"You owe me big time, brother, for bringing the woman of your dreams into your life," Riya teased.

"I guess so."

"Now, get off my screen because I want to talk to my future sister-in-law, and if she agrees, potentially my business partner," Riya cheered, and Seema smiled, sending silent prayers to the heavens for her blessings.

Later that night, she lay in Raghav's arms enjoying the sound of his beating heart against her cheek. She still could not believe how life changed in a matter of a few months. Everything she had hoped for in her life was in front of her. It was as if everything was bundled into one gift and left for her to discover.

"I just can't believe where I am right now," she whispered.

He pulled her closer to him. "How did I get so lucky?"

She snuggled closer to him. "Silly man. I will miss you when you go out of town tomorrow."

He moved, nuzzling her neck. "You have no idea, but I need to make this one last trip, so I can get everything set up in Malaysia. Then, I will come back home to you after a boring day at work to get my butt kicked at the games."

"I'll miss you, but it will give me time to spend with Nandu. She is pissed you are taking away her roommate," Seema teased.

"Baby, you have no idea what it feels to find the missing piece of the puzzle, and I don't just mean figuratively." He laughed and added, "We need to compete with puzzle-making as well while you are beating me at every game."

She smiled. "I can say you are my missing piece, a boulder-sized one that makes me whole. The first time we kissed, I knew I was home, and I didn't need to look for a family that I probably don't have."

He kissed the top of her head. "If you want to look, you should."

"I haven't checked on the research in weeks. I just—" She pulled back to look at him. "You are my everything, and I don't know what else would make me happier."

He smiled, his lips brushing over hers. "You complete me, Seema."

23

"Don't look so devastated just because you have to come stay with me," Nandu teased as Seema looked at her screen, perplexed, a couple of days after Raghav left for a business trip.

Seema rolled her eyes. "Not funny. Cut it out."

Nandu laughed. "You have turned into a ball of mush lately."

"Nandu, I still can't make heads or tails of these events." She pointed at the document Nandu had sent about the Rayudu's anniversary party.

"I still can't figure out what they want us to do. The brothers keep changing the plan because they don't want their parents to know about the surprise."

Seema thought for a moment. "Our goal was to support the brothers. They should stick to a final plan, so we can start implementing."

"I don't know about that."

"You need to help them make those decisions, Nandu."

Nandu snickered. "Why don't you deal with the brothers? They have an idea, a surprise party, and that's it."

"Nandu, I thought you wanted to lead this effort."

"I don't know if I should be leading the effort."

"What? Why?"

"I don't think the brothers like me because I told them they need to get their act together." Nandu shrugged.

"Nandu, we talked about this. We need to provide feedback in a constructive way."

"Yup. Like I said, you should deal with them until they have their plan sorted out, especially the little brother. He sure is a fireball." Nandu laughed, making Seema glare at her.

"I think—"

Seema looked away when her phone started to ring. Mr. Sangha was calling her back. She had reached out earlier in the week to tell him to halt the research. "Let me take this. I'll need a few minutes. Just sit tight."

"Go for it." Nandu pulled her laptop closed to her as they sat across from each other in Seema's office.

"Hello, Mr. Sangha. How are you?"

"Seema, sorry I could not get back to you sooner. I wanted to wait until I had some confirmation."

"Not a problem at all, sir. I had called to let you know that I'm okay with halting the research since we had not seen many matches." Seema caught the surprise in Nandu's eyes in response to her words and mouthed, *Whaaat,* rather dramatically.

"Seema, I am calling because we have a definite match for your DNA."

"Oh." She was taken aback. She realized it was not the reaction she had imagined she would have when she had a positive report from the research.

"Because of the identity of the person, I have asked my team to run the match thrice, and we have received a confirmation of the closest relative, one of your parents."

Seema's breath started to come fast, and she was glad Nandu decided to step out of her office at that time. "Who is this person?”

“Seema, my team has been able to identify your father as Devaraj Rayudu.”

Seema wasn’t sure if she heard the name right. “Do you mean… the upcoming political leader of theJanatha Seva Party?”

She was still in shock of the truth as Mr. Sangha continued to talk about the process they used to confirm for sure. Instead of being happy about the revelation, she wanted to know why she grew up as an orphan. ‘Thank you… Mr. Sangha.”

“You are welcome, Seema.” The older man paused for a moment and added, “You had a parental match with Mr. Rayudu but not his wife.”

“I… I don’t understand.” She was confused.

“Seema, you are like my daughter, and it pains to tell me that based on the timing of when his older son was born and your birthdate, you are a child from another woman who we have not been able to trace or identify.”

Her worst nightmare was coming true. She was an unwanted child. It explained a lot of things, and she sat frozen as Mr. Sangha waited as if to help her process the last detail he shared. “Thank you for clarifying, Mr. Sangha.”

“You are welcome, Seema. And the research results are confidential, and only my core team is aware of the details. I will send you the match results, and I will let you decide how to handle the communication.” Mr. Sangha ended the call leaving her mind reeling with the new revelation.

“That’s breaking news that you want to stop the search,” Nandu said, cutting through her state of daze a short while later.

Seema looked at her friend, trying hard to blink away her tears and the need to fall to the floor and curl up to handle the pain deep inside. She looked aimlessly as Nandu came back to sit on the chair. "Has Raghav had anything to do with your decision not to go after the search?"

Seema was out of breath, and she was sweating all over. She excused herself and stepped out of her office. She went straight to the back of the building where there was a small patch of greenery and dialed Raghav's number.

His phone rang for a moment before being sent to his voicemail.

Raghav: *In a meeting. All okay?*

"No," she whispered as tears gathered in her eyes, and she looked up at the sky. "This is not what I wanted."

The words she vocalized was a possibility that she had considered, but it was not as easy to absorb as she had thought it would be. She knew the happiness of knowing her roots would trump any harsh truth that was related to her birth, but it was harder to accept the fact that the man had a family who was being portrayed as the most ideal in society. She would have preferred a parent who had given her up because of poverty or any other reason, but not this.

An unwanted and most likely an illegitimate child if her DNA didn't match the man's wife as the parent. Seema could not deny that Nandu was right about not knowing the truth and accepting the fact that she didn't have anyone, but the new revelation was definitely harder to digest.

Now what? She knew who they were, and there was no way she was going to reach out. If she was unwanted as a child, what would have changed? Could she accept the new piece of information as a fact and not think about the family or their reasons for not wanting her?

Later that night, she was curled up in bed, traces of dried-up tears on her cheeks when Nandu knocked on her door. She lay still pretending to be asleep, not having the ability or the energy to speak to anyone. She left the office, unable to handle the turmoil in her head. It was devastating to realize that she was given up by choice, and that made tears roll down her cheeks, however much she tried to tell herself she didn't care. The man she loved was all she needed for her to be happy.

Seema could hear Nandu speak right outside her door. "Yeah, she is here in her room sleeping. I'll have her call you back."

Nandu had to be speaking to Raghav, and just the very thought of him made her break into uncontrollable sobs as she hid her face into her pillow.

"Seema, you up?" Nandu asked as she walked into her room. "Raghav wants to talk to you."

Seema sat up and took Nandu's hand, gesturing for her to sit on the bed next to her. She knew it was time to share the news that she had been bitter about all day. Maybe it was the best way to get it off her chest.

"Raghav..."

"Baby, what's wrong? Are you okay?"

Seema's worries started to melt when she heard his voice. "I'm okay. Just a bad headache and I fell asleep."

"I got worried when you didn't answer your phone and called Nandu." His voice was weak.

"I'm okay. My phone is probably in my purse somewhere." She let out a laugh and looked at Nandu who had a questioning look on her face.

"What's going on?" he asked like he knew she wanted to talk.

"Raghav, I am going to put you on speaker, so I can tell Nandu also what is bothering me."

"Okay," Raghav said, and Nandu interjected, "You are really being weird right now."

"I got a call from Mr. Sangha, and they were able to identify who my father is."

Nandu blinked for a second and let out a sequel, hugging Seema. "Why didn't you tell me? That is such good news. Who is it?"

Seema shook her head as she looked at the phone, realizing Raghav had not said anything. "Raghav and Nandu, I want to drop it here because I wanted to know who my family is, and I know."

Nandu looked at Seema like she was crazy. "Really?"

Seema nodded, and Raghav said, "Whatever you wish to do, it is your decision."

"No, Raghav. Don't encourage this. I know she will keep thinking about it again." Nandu knew her very well.

"If she decides to reach out to her father at a later point, then it is her choice." Raghav's voice was stern.

Nandu wasn't ready to let go. "Are you sure about this?"

"Yes, let it go." Seema was firm about her decision. At that point, after spending the entire afternoon mulling over how a family could not want her, she painfully accepted the harsh truth.

"I'll leave right after my meeting tomorrow," Raghav said, and Seema took him off the speaker to talk in private.

"No, Raghav. Please finish your work and then leave." Seema blew a kiss to her friend as she left the room to give Seema and Raghav some privacy.

"Nothing is more important than you. I was worried when I could not reach you all afternoon."

"I'm sorry. I had hoped that the happiness from finding a relative would surpass any harsh truth around my birth, but knowing that this man is portrayed to have the perfect family was far too painful."

Raghav was silent for a moment. "So, I take it that this man is a public figure?"

"Yes. One other reason I don't want to contact him because they will see no good in me reaching out. I want nothing from them. I have everything I need. You."

"I love you, too, baby. I'll see you tomorrow."

"I miss you, Raghav."

"Get some sleep, love."

She ended the call and lay in bed wondering about the man who was projected to be the future leader of the state and potentially the country someday. And to top it all, she had a contract in place to manage the anniversary event. Could she do it now?

She took a deep breath and told herself to be professional. Her goal was not to let anyone get under her skin if it were a man who most likely cheated on his wife who doted on him for the ideal man he portrays himself as.

He may have been a bad husband but was considered a true leader, so she decided to keep her personal issues with the man away from her work.

24

The next morning, Seema spent almost an hour convincing Raghav to finish his work in Malaysia, so he didn't have to go back again. She was glad he agreed, although she would have wanted to curl up in his arms and enjoy his warmth and comfort.

She had all night to think over the new piece of information about her identity and realized it was likely her biological father didn't know she existed. If the woman who was her mother never told him, he would never know. If he didn't know, it was best to keep it buried, especially when he was trying to do something good for the people.

Whatever the case, she decided to move on with her life like the information would not change anything for her. Absolutely nothing.

She was in the middle of reviewing the party plan for the weekend-long anniversary celebration for the man in the upcoming weeks while trying really hard not to think of him as her father.

She smiled when she heard her phone ring and saw it was Raghav. "Mr. Vasudev, why aren't you working and letting me work?"

"Because I can't stop thinking of you."

"Very sweet, but I have an anniversary party to plan."

"You are such a workaholic," he teased.

"I hope you said that while looking in the mirror." She chuckled.

"I can't wait to see you—"

Seema interjected when she saw Sravan talking to her assistant outside her office. "Raghav, I got to go."

"No, wait." He laughed.

"I'm sorry, baby... I have to..." She looked up as Sravan opened the door loudly and stepped into her office.

"Hi, Sravan, what a pleasant surprise. I wasn't expecting you." She tried to forget that the man standing in front of her was her half-brother.

"Is that so, Seema? You weren't very pleasant in the letter you sent to the party office."

Seema was confused. "I'm sorry. I don't understand. Are you here to talk about the plan for the anniversary party?"

"Will you stop pretending? It is fucking annoying. Just get to the point."

Seema looked at him and said in a firm tone, "I am not sure what you are talking about."

"Fine. Your contract for the anniversary party is canceled. And I am in the process of getting your business license revoked as well."

"What?" She was taken aback.

"Who do you think you are messing with? If you think you can extort money with a fake DNA test, you are the stupidest woman on the face of this earth."

"Sravan, what are you talking about?"

He pulled out a crumpled sheet of paper out of his pocket and tossed it on the table in front of her. "I'm sure you'll enjoy what you wrote."

Her heart sank when she read the letter addressed to Mr. Rayudu with a copy of the DNA test result, her name on it, and the letter attached threatening to reveal the details to the media if the mentioned ransom in cash was not dropped off at a location to be disclosed over the phone.

She dropped the letter on the table and said, "I had nothing to do with this."

"I spoke to the department head of the institute that performed the research, and he confirmed that you had requested the DNA match."

Seema shook her head. "Yes, I was the one who requested the research, but this letter, that's not me."

"Mr. Sangha confirmed that you were the only one who received the information. So, who else would care to use this information?"

"I don't know." She could not believe what he was saying.

"Listen to me carefully. You are messing with the wrong family. I will not tolerate this bullshit. Who the heck gave you permission to check my parents' DNA? I am going to file a lawsuit against you."

"The research is approved and funded by the government. I was merely a subject that they performed their research on, and it took the approval of a high-court judge for the details to be revealed to me if a match was found."

"Looks like you have been planning this for a long time. You can go to the media or do whatever, you will not be getting a single penny."

He started to walk away, and she tried hard not to yell back, but she did. "I don't need the money. You better stop the real people who are behind this blackmail if you care for your father's image."

Sravan stopped and turned to look at her. "That's right, you don't need the money. It looks like you bagged a big fish."

She was furious, but she took a deep breath and said, "Please watch what you say."

"You don't deserve any respect. You will be hearing from my lawyers for these wrong allegations."

"And what will you do when you find out I am your father's daughter?" she spat.

"Impossible. My father is the most loyal man. These allegations are to take a dig at him as he is gaining popularity. Be ready to go to jail for blackmail." He stormed off, leaving her shaking all over.

She took a deep breath and told herself there was probably a good reason why she grew up as an orphan than amongst men who are cheaters and others who didn't know how to respect women.

Seema let out a huff, not wanting to let any sadness get to her and decided she was better off being angry rather than upset. She sat back on the chair, shaking all over when she heard the door to her office open, and Nandu walked in, looking rather angry.

"What was that about?"

Seema shook her head not wanting to discuss any of the conversation as she replayed the words. Sravan was so sure the DNA test was bogus, it made her question the result. Could it have been a mistake?

She ignored Nandu's questioning looks and dialed Mr. Sangha. "Sir, do you have a few minutes to talk?"

"Yes, Seema." The man sounded apologetic and scared at the same time. "I have not sent the results to anyone but you, and no one other than my team had the details. I am trying to figure out how someone was using it for ransom."

"Sir, I am sorry for causing all the trouble."

"Seema. Not at all. I have an internal investigation running to check how the information was leaked."

"Please do what it takes to keep this from the media. No matter what happened decades ago, the people need a leader, a good one."

Mr. Sangha let out a sigh. "If we could get more and more people to think like you, we would have a different future for the country."

Seema ended the call and looked at Nandu. "I will tell you everything, but you are not to repeat any of this anywhere. Promise me."

She told Nandu everything, and as she told her about what Sravan spoke about, she knew it was going to be a messy affair. She was going to give it a day and reach out to Sravan again to sort things out in an amicable manner. She knew it would be an embarrassment for the entire family, especially the way it was portrayed in the blackmail letter and to the party members if the news were to come out. As her client, she felt responsible for protecting their privacy.

"You are nuts even to think about them after what Sravan said to you. We can hire lawyers, too. They agreed to a contract, and he can't just decide to cancel it because of his wish and will."

"Nandu, keep this to yourself, please."

"How do you feel about finding your family?" Nandu asked after a long period of silence.

She took a deep breath. "I was hoping to be happy about finding my roots, but I feel indifferent. Like I don't care for any of it now. All I need is Raghav."

"Did you tell him about all this?"

Seema shook her head. "He is in meetings all day, and I don't know if I should tell him yet. I want to be able to handle this mess myself."

*****

Later that evening, Seema was in the office working on a plan just so she could keep herself distracted from everything when she heard the door to her office open.

"Nandu, I thought—" Her voice was lost in a squeal of joy when she saw Raghav stand by the door. His beautiful smile lit up her heart, and everything that she had been thinking of melted away.

"Raghav, you told me you were staying for a couple more days." She hugged him before pulling back to kiss him on his lips.

He held her to him, his lips brushing over hers eagerly. "I missed you, baby."

"I'm so happy you are back. Were you able to get everything taken care of?"

He shrugged. "I guess I'll need to go back, but the next time I am going to go back with my fiancée."

She smiled. "I could use another break, I guess."

He ran his lips on her cheek and said, "Let's go home."

Seema sat in the car as they drove through traffic debating if she should tell Raghav about everything that happened.

"What's going on, baby?"

"There have been more developments from the research, and it has gotten so messy. I... I don't know if I should talk about it."

"Why wouldn't you want to talk about it now?"

She smiled. "I'm just so happy you are back, I just don't want to think about it."

"But what if it's going to nag you all night."

She took in a deep breath. "This whole thing is going to nag me for the rest of my life. It has been harder than I expected to handle the truth."

"I can't let you feel that way, love."

She shrugged. "I guess there is no way around it. I know I'll be bitter about everything."

He let out a hissy breath. "No matter what happened in the past, you should not feel that way, and most of all, what I will not tolerate is someone talking to you like that."

Seema looked at Raghav, not knowing what he was referring to as she had not shared any of the conversations from that day with him. "Raghav, I—"

"I don't care who they are, no one gets to talk to you like that." He let out an angry huff.

"How—"

"I heard every word of what he said because the call did not end when you put your phone away this morning."

"I... I don't know how to..." Her words were lost when he turned off of the road onto a driveway that led to a small lane with residential buildings. "Where are we?"

Raghav came around and helped her out of the car and led her up the stairs to the front door after checking in with the security at the main gate. "We are here to meet Mr. Rayudu."

She stopped abruptly. "No. Let's not do this."

He stopped to look at her. "You are not here to claim an inheritance or a social status but the respect you deserve for the woman you are. The tone he took with you made my blood boil."

"It's such a mess already. We should go back."

He took a deep breath. "If there isn't any other way to address it other than talking through this, we can leave."

She thought for a moment. "I don't know if I can do this, but..."

Raghav waited as she thought through it. "I will do whatever it takes for your happiness."

Seema let out a sigh and said, "I want to get this over with once in for all. If they didn't know I existed, they will tonight, and after that, I don't care what happens."

Raghav pressed his lips together as he led her to the main door where a security guard was stationed. "We have an appointment with Mr. Rayudu."

The man led them to the side of the house to a separate space that was set up as a meeting space with a few couches.

"Who are we meeting now?"

"Mr. Rayudu, the leader."

They sat next to each other and waited for the man to arrive, and her anxiety started to grow. "I never want to deal with these people after I finish the anniversary event."

"Seriously? You will do their event?"

Seema nodded. "I'm a professional, and I have a job to do unless they cancel the contract."

"You are unbelievable." He chuckled.

"Now, if they cancel the contract and don't pay, I'm going to court."

"I heard that—" He looked away when they heard footsteps.

A man Seema had seen many times on television and on the billboards around the city but never in person appeared before them. The way the man looked at her like he cared for her and the warmth the genuine smile exuded, she smiled back.

"Raghav, it is so good to meet you again."

"Thank you for taking the time to meet with me at such short notice. This is my fiancée, Seema." Raghav nodded.

"Nice to meet you, Seema. What brings you here tonight, Raghav?"

"Mr. Rayudu, we met a couple of months ago, and I pledged my support to your campaign. The reason I did that is because this young lady recommended that everyone support you in any way possible." The older man smiled at Seema, and Raghav added, "And it now saddens me to tell you that I will be withdrawing my support."

25

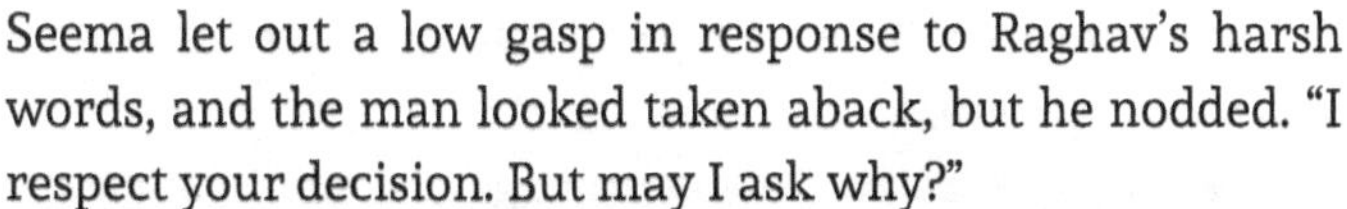

Seema let out a low gasp in response to Raghav's harsh words, and the man looked taken aback, but he nodded. "I respect your decision. But may I ask why?"

"The reason is your campaign manager insulted my fiancée, and I will not support anyone who disrespects the woman I love."

The man seemed shocked. "You mean Sravan?"

"Yes."

"What happened? How can I make this right? Not to gain your support back, but I cannot tolerate any disrespect to women."

Seema was surprised by the genuine anger and disappointment in his eyes.

Was this man a good actor?

"I suggest that you speak to your son about what happened. My request is that he apologize to Seema. He knows where to find us." Raghav stood up as if to leave, and the man gestured them to wait.

"I will have this sorted out right now." The man made a call and instructed someone to have his younger son meet him immediately.

"Please. He will be here in a few minutes. Can I offer you something to drink?" The man seemed so nice, Seema was starting to feel bad about putting him in a tough spot.

"We should go," she whispered.

Raghav nodded. "We unfortunately can't wait. We need to go."

As they got up to leave, they heard footsteps, and Sravan appeared at the doorway. "Papa, you wanted to see me?"

"You know, Raghav and his fiancée, Seema."

"Yes." Sravan glared at Seema.

"Sravan, I am not sure what happened, but I am disappointed to hear you were disrespectful to Seema."

Sravan averted his eyes from his father to her. "How dare you show up here, and—"

Raghav interjected. "If you don't get a grip of your tone, it will not be pleasant for you."

"You brought your billionaire henchman to threaten me?" Sravan barked.

Seema felt the anger from that morning snowball into something uncontrollable, and she reached out to strike him across his cheek with her palm. The sound of flesh-on-flesh shocked Sravan as he rubbed his cheek absentmindedly. "Watch what you say about my fiancé."

"Sravan. Behave yourself." His father looked appalled.

"Papa, you have no idea what she has done."

Raghav stepped in. "Yes, he doesn't know why you stormed into Seema's office because she chose not to disclose it, not even to me. I'm only here to let your father know that I am withdrawing my support because of how Seema was insulted by you."

"We don't care for your support, buzz off." Sravan's anger was out of control.

The leader who was shocked to see the behavior, raised his voice. "I need to know what happened. Raghav, please. This is unacceptable behavior from my son, but I need to understand what happened."

"Papa, don't listen to their bullshit."

"Sravan," the man commanded, and the young man fell silent.

"Raghav and Seema, please sit down. More than losing your support, I am saddened by this behavior."

"I'm sorry I raised my hand at your child." Seema felt embarrassed.

"He, indeed, behaved like a child." The man looked at his son standing by the door fuming and added, "Would you please tell me what happened?"

Raghav looked at Seema and said, "Only if you want to."

Seema looked at the man who had sadness and embarrassment in his eyes for his son's behavior. She took a deep breath and said, "Mr. Rayudu, I had no intention of sharing this information or use it for other means, but according to a DNA match performed by a research institute, my DNA matches with yours. You and I are related."

The man looked at her, perplexed like he didn't see what the big deal was, and she continued. "The percentage of match indicates that you are my father, and since my DNA did not have the parental match with your wife—"

"Stop it. Stop all this bullshit. Papa, don't listen to them. They are trying to pin this on you for political gain."

The man looked shocked as moisture seemed to gather in his eyes, and his voice shook when he spoke, "Sravan, go. Bring your mother."

"Papa, what are you talking about? Even if a mistake was made, Ma doesn't need to know." Sravan looked horrified, and Seema was shocked to see the man's response. She had expected to see guilt or anger but not surprise. Like he could not believe he heard what Seema told him, in a good way.

"Sravan, now. Go get your mother."

Sravan ran his fingers through his hair, unable to figure out what to do, but like a good son, he left them alone. The man turned slowly to look at Seema and then at Raghav.

"Raghav, I owe you my life for bringing Seema with you," he said and turned to look at Seema. "Never in a million years did I think that this day would—"

The man lost his voice, and he started to weep as he sat on the sofa like he could not stand. The sight in front of her made Seema's stomach churn, and her chest tightened like there was a weight placed on her in response to the sadness the man seemed to be facing.

As if on instinct, she kneeled next to him and placed her hand on the man's shoulder. "Sir, I'm sorry. I didn't mean to hurt anyone by searching for a relative. I only wanted to know my roots. I'm not here to disrupt a family."

The man kept his eyes downcast as he took off his glasses and wiped his eyes with a handkerchief. "You are my child, and I don't know what I did to be blessed with this moment."

Seema was surprised to hear the man's voice. Did that mean she was not an unwanted child?

"Deva, what is going on?" A woman's voice made Seema look up and saw that Sravan and his brother, Varun, had joined them.

Seema stepped away as the woman kneeled in front of the man as if to console him, so she went to stand by Raghav. "I'm feeling very sad about this. I should not have dug up all of this."

"You didn't do anything wrong." He leaned over to kiss her on the cheek.

Seema stood by Raghav watching Mr. Rayudu and his wife speak quietly, and he said something to her that made her let out a sob and look at Seema.

Seema didn't know what to say as the woman stood up to walk to her, tears rolling down her cheek. The woman cupped her hands on Seema's cheek and said, "I can't believe this." She turned back to look at her husband. "She has her eyes."

Mr. Rayudu stood up to walk over to where his wife stood by Seema and slowly took her hand in his. "Seema, you are my daughter. My child, who I never thought survived the flash floods when I lost your mother. She was pregnant with you, and I didn't think you—"

The woman hugged her and started to weep, and Seema was taken aback by the emotional display that rattled her on the inside.

Was the couple actually happy to see her? What did the man mean by *your* mother? Who was the woman who was in the room?

"Can someone explain to me what happened?" Sravan demanded, frustrated.

Seema looked up to find Sravan red with anger, but his older brother was looking at her like he could not believe his eyes. Varun moved toward his father and put an arm around him. The man looked at his oldest son and patted his shoulder. "Your sister came looking for us."

"Papa don't believe her. The DNA test is fake. She is a fraudster. She is trying to prove that you have been with another woman."

Mr. Rayudu's wife looked at her son. "Sravan, if there is another woman in your father's life, that would be me. This girl here is your sister. Varun and this girl are his children from your father's first wife, who we lost in a tragedy. His first wife is also my older sister, who he loved very much."

"What?" Sravan looked lost.

"We got married so I could be a mother to Varun and for your father to learn to love me and give me a child... I'm living my sister's life. This happiness and the family were what my sister left for me after losing my entire family in the floods. I am the reason she is not with us anymore, and yet, I was given everything to be happy about today."

"Ma, what are you saying?" Sravan walked over to his mother, looking guilty.

"Sravan, you are named after my sister Sravani. She sacrificed her life to save Varun and me during the flash floods. I was the one who wanted to go checkout the riverside and when the water surge came, we saw my sister and parents be washed away in the current. We knew we had lost all of them and the baby when the search party came back with no trace of either of them."

Seema had her eyes downcast as she clung to Raghav, not able to process any of the new information.

"Seema," she heard Sravan say, and she looked up to find him looking heartbroken. "I... I'm sorry. I was so wrapped up in the idea that someone was looking to find dirt on my father..." he paused, "... our father that I didn't even think for a minute that you could be my sister."

Seema was overwhelmed with everything she heard and buried her face into Raghav's arm. "I can't take this. I don't know what is going on."

"Seema, look at your family. This is what you wanted." He smiled, looking up at her family members.

Mr. Rayudu stepped close to Seema, taking her hand in his. "Seema, this may all be a lot to process, but I am beyond thrilled that you looked for us. We are your family. Will you please accept us as yours?"

She smiled, nodding, unable to talk.

Mr. Rayudu took her into his arms and said, "Since your little brother insulted you, should we put him up for adoption?"

Seema laughed as Sravan hugged her and her father. "I'm so sorry, Seema."

"I'm sorry I slapped you."

"I needed it." He chuckled, looking at his older brother while his mother shed tears of joy. "But, I'm pissed no one told me all this."

Seema chuckled. "You are not alone. I just found out myself."

Mr. Rayudu loosened his hold on Seema, and Sravan to walk toward Raghav. He took Raghav's hand in his and said, "While you came here to tell me you are pulling back your support, you brought me my biggest strength today, Raghav. I will be indebted to you for the rest of my life. What can I give you in return?"

"I only ask your daughter's hand in marriage, and we are even." Raghav let out a laugh and shook his future father-in-law's hand.

Seema stood in the middle of the room surrounded by the family she had cared for all her life but didn't know, but the man who stood by her father was her everything. The moment she was in was a gift Raghav gave her that she would have never taken herself.

She looked at the man she would love to eternity, the one thing that filled the crater inside her and now, she was presented with a beautiful life.

Later that night, Seema laughed as they drove back to his apartment from the Rayudus' residence. "I just can't believe what happened tonight. Just amazing. I have two brothers... two."

Raghav smiled, keeping his eyes on the road. "I'm happy for you, sweetheart. I thought you might end up staying at your parents' place."

"No way. I want to be where you are, and Raghav, I love you so much for taking me there because I don't know if I would have ever thought of facing him."

Raghav was silent for a long moment. "How are you taking the news about the mother you lost?"

"I... it's a miracle I am alive. The fact that I was born premature based on what my father said was not recorded anywhere. The guilt my mother's sister held all these years for being the reason for her sister falling and getting swept away in the flash flood, I never imagined such happy families had so much sadness."

"It's unfortunate what happened and how it happened."

Seema tsked. "I don't know how Varun felt when he was told about his biological mother."

"Varun was too young, and I think your mother's sister raised him as her own."

"I'm so happy, and whoever that person was who sent the blackmail letter, looks like my father is going to thank them in front of the media."

"It had to be an amateur who figured they could make a quick buck out of it, but I'm sure the department will find them soon," Raghav scoffed.

She fell silent for a moment like something just hit her. "I just realized I have an anniversary party to plan for my parents."

Raghav laughed. "You are unbelievable."

"Are you and Riya working together going forward?"

"Yes. We are, and we are going to have a blast..." she said and added giggling, "... and I have two unmarried brothers I need to take care of their weddings, too."

"What about our wedding?" he asked as he pulled the car into the underground parking space.

She blushed. "I can't wait to marry you."

He ran his arm around her as they stepped into the elevator. "Do you feel like getting married tonight? We can elope, just say the words."

"Raghav, don't do that. I promised your mom we won't do that."

Raghav chuckled. "I would be breaking tradition if we didn't elope."

She quickly stepped out of the elevator and ran to the main door punching in the code. "I'm not eloping with you."

He caught her by her waist as they stepped indoors, and he shut the door behind him as he swept her off the floor to pull her lips to his. He walked them to what has lately become their favorite rendezvous point in the house, his lips sucking hers hungrily. "I missed you, sweetheart."

"Me, too," she mumbled against his lips eagerly tangling her tongue with his.

His hands slid up her thighs pushing her dress up to bunch around her hips as his fingers found the molten heat between her legs. He ran his fingertips over the wet spot on her panties, making her shudder.

His lips left hers as she caught her breath and trailed south, nipping her skin along the way, his fingers expertly rolling the zipper down on the back of her dress. He pulled her dress off her shoulders to take her yearning breast in his hand to squeeze it delectably, making her moan.

The pleasure waves were building up as he moved closer to her epicenter, and when he kneeled in front of her, she clenched her inner folds in anticipation. She let out a low gasp when he yanked her panties down before spreading her knees apart to take her with him to ride the wave of desire. She crashed in his arms, satiated by his touch as they surged together.

Every time he made love to her, she swore she saw fireworks behind her eyelids, and she only knew to collapse in his arms, holding onto him, never to let him go.

Later that night, they lay in each other's arms, satiated and tired. He planted kisses along her arm. "What are you thinking about, love?"

"I was thinking about how in a matter of a few weeks, my life changed completely, and I am hoping this is not a dream."

He kissed the back of her hand, causing her to smile. She blushed, and the next moment, he sunk his teeth into her skin, making her yelp.

"Raghav," she growled, pulling her hand away.

He laughed, pulling her back to him, kissing the nape of her neck. "Feels pretty real, huh, baby?"

"Not funny." She giggled.

"This is what you wanted, love."

She turned to face him. "Yes, the family is what I wanted, but you are what I needed. I don't think I would be this happy if I didn't have you and your love."

He brushed his lips over hers, and she smiled. "I love you, baby."

<h1 style="text-align:center">Epilogue</h1>

Five Years Later...

"Why do you look so nervous?" Raghav ran his lips over Seema's temple as he whispered.

Seema squeezed his hand, her eyes on the family and friends gathered for her parents' anniversary party, the event she had been putting together for her parents from the time she was reunited with the family. "It's going to be emotional for me to see Ma and Papa's expression, and I hope they like it."

"Baby, what you are about to do for them is just amazing, and it's going to be beautiful," Raghav assured.

"They have no idea, and the guests don't either. I am having second thoughts about how the media will portray this now that he is the Chief Minister."

"No one will know. It's our immediate families and close friends."

"True." She smiled as she scanned the area filled with the large families on her parents' and Raghav's side. Who knew she would go from zero family to thousands of relatives and friends and an endless amount of love from the man who she loved with all her heart?

"What if Ma and Papa don't like it?"

"Why won't they?"

She turned to look at the stage's generic background that was set up for the event to see how it had changed with the props as her parents came walking into the party hall and added, "I think I should cancel this."

"No, you won't. This is such a beautiful thought. You do know there are a few cultures who do this when a man turns sixty, and in many other countries, this is like renewing wedding vows. It's not like this is a full-on wedding ceremony. They will exchange garlands, and the guests can bless them."

"Yes, but I am so nervous." She looked at the traditionally decked-up stage that would transform into a setup to perform a wedding ceremony for her parents, the couple who tied the knot on paper during a sad and traumatic phase of their life after losing a loved one.

Seema had found out while looking through family pictures that there was no wedding picture of her father and the woman he loved, the God-sent mother of his three children. She planned a traditional wedding ceremony for them and had only shared the idea with her immediate family. Her father's five sisters were going to accompany him to the stage like how a groom is brought to the wedding pavilion, while her mother would be escorted by her brothers and cousins, a beautiful sheer curtain lit with tiny LEDs, so the groom could not see her until after they have exchanged the flower garlands. She was most nervous about her mother's reaction to the setup. It was not a traditional ceremony but a way for her mother to enjoy the wedding-themed party.

"I have a surprise for you tonight," he said, almost in an attempt to distract her.

"Stop. It's not helping."

"I'm serious. We are leaving on a trip tonight," he whispered, his breath hot in her ear.

She turned to look into his eyes. "You are kidding."

"We leave from here, right after your parents' party."

She smiled. "Really?"

"Yes, now enjoy your favorite event."

She leaned her back into him as she turned away to face the guests. "My favorite event is our wedding."

Seema was thrilled to be blessed with the beautiful wedding she had wished for, and it was in her most favorite place—Raghav's family ancestral home with family and friends. Her next favorite was her older brother, Varun, when he married his high school sweetheart. It was Sravan's turn, and she was thrilled her little brother shared his intentions to propose to a woman he had met on a vacation very soon.

"You wanna get married again?" He chuckled.

"Sure, anytime." She smiled up at him, fighting the need to kiss him.

"Good. We sneak out right after this wedding and go get married." He laughed.

"Don't be silly. We are not leaving without our baby." She looked away from him to look at their three-year-old daughter, who had the entire family wrapped around her little finger. Everyone adored and spoiled her.

"She doesn't care about us as long as she has her grandma around." Raghav chuckled, making Seema smile, watching their daughter sit with Raghav's mom. The two were inseparable, and Seema thanked the heavens for the blessings their child had in the form of family.

"Seema, they have arrived, and we got them separated to enter from two different sides." Nandu's words made her even more nervous, but a new excitement started, and she could not wait to see her parents' delight. Nandu, who had wanted to volunteer with the Janatha Seva Party,ended up working for her Seema's father.

"You got this, sweetheart. They will love it." Raghav's words gave her the assurance she needed in that moment.

She stood next to Raghav on one side of the stage, but she could see both entrances. She held Raghav's hand as she looked toward the entrances with bated breath.

The musicians started beating the drums according to their instructions as soon as her parents came into sight, and she saw the expression on her father's face first when he looked at her like he suspected something. She waved at him as he waited with his sisters in tow as her mother stepped into the space. The moment her mother did so, her brothers and other family members held the screen which caused her to let out a laugh, and immediately she knew Seema was up to something.

Seema blew her mother a kiss as Nandu handed her the decorated green coconut that was tradition for the bride to hold in her hands as she walked to the wedding pavilion. Tears gathered in her eyes when she saw her mother let out a sob and look at Seema even as her brothers hugged their mother.

"Look, they are so happy," Raghav said while Seema tried hard to contain her happy tears.

Nandu directed the bride's group as Riya joined Seema's aunts for some fun as they walked alongside her father toward the stage.

Seema turned away from her parents to look at the stage that was on the last steps to be set up as a traditionally decorated wedding pavilion—the garlands and the beautiful silk fabric decorated with flowers.

"I'm so proud of you, love. You should go to your parents."

She hugged his arm. "I want to be here and watch them."

Seema wiped away the tears of joy that refused to stop as she watched her parents walk up the stage from the two sides. Her mother was on the side where she stood, and as she got closer, Seema reached out to hug her brothers before hugging her mother. "I hope you like this theme for your anniversary party, Ma."

"Sweetheart, how did I get so lucky?"

Varun chuckled. "We all did, Ma."

Seema kissed her mother and said, "Let's go. We can't keep the groom waiting."

Seema walked with her mother to where her father sat, overwhelmed, and hugged him. "Papa, you are such a handsome groom and the most loved man in our state."

Her father laughed and kissed his daughter on her forehead. Seema looked at her mother as she sat next to her husband. "I love you both. You can yell at me later if I embarrassed you, but you two need this for the loving couple you are and will be for years to come.

"Deva, she is the best gift you have ever given me." Her mother was emotional as she held Seema's hand in hers.

Her father nodded. "Seema, you are the light of our life. God bless you with everything you ever wish for."

"Thank you, Papa. Now, time to tie the knot with Ma, again."

Later that night, she walked a step behind Raghav as he led her out of the large banquet hall where the reception for her parents was held after the wedding.

"Raghav, were you serious about leaving tonight? I still need to pack."

"Do not worry, my love. You are covered."

"Who did you scheme with for this?" she asked as he ushered her into the back of a waiting limousine before getting into the vehicle.

He kissed her hard on her lips. "I've been waiting to do this all evening."

She kissed him back. "Me, too."

"Are you ready?"

He chuckled. "For a one-week getaway with your husband?"

She widened her eyes, unable to believe her ears. She knew he was in the middle of a critical venture and could not take time off for a few months. "Really?"

He smiled, brushing his lips over hers. "Baby, didn't you say you wanted me to take a break when you take yours?"

"You are kidding."

"You know how seriously I take my wife's wishes. Her wish is my command" He nibbled on her ear, making her giggle.

"Where are we headed?"

"The jet is waiting, and you tell me where you want to go for our honeymoon number... I lost count."

She let out a squeal of joy. "For real? The entire week?"

"Pick the place, love."

She narrowed her eyes, making him shudder in response to the fire in her eyes. "Paris, baby. I want to be in the city of love with my sweet husband."

He pulled her into a kiss, and she melted in his arms. He made her heart flutter every time his lips conquered hers, her stomach clenched in anticipation as her blood coursed through her veins setting her on fire. His gentle touch could keep her warm in the arctic tundra, and the very look in his eyes made her feel like the most beautiful woman in the world.

"I love you, Raghav... forever."

"Baby, you are my everything. Nothing makes sense without you."

She smiled as he pulled her into an embrace that held the promise to love and protect her forever, and she didn't know when the man she knew as **Brozilla, *The Bride's Brother*** became the king of her heart.

The END

Author's Note

Thank you for choosing to spend your time with Raghav and Seema. I hope you enjoyed reading *The Bride's Brother* as much as I did writing their love story.

Due to the pandemic, I missed attending a lot of weddings, and I wrote this story, so I can enjoy the fun of being with family and friends, while thinking about the events. I have no skills as a wedding planner and all the events are what I thought would be fun to have for someone's wedding.

I hope you were able to get to escape if you had missed on attending the weddings just like me.

I would like to ask you to rate/review this book on Amazon and Goodreads as it will help me know what you, my readers, would like to see in future stories.

Thank you,

P.G. Van

Email: pgvanpublish@gmail.com

Connect with me on Instagram (@Authorpgvan) and on Facebook for the latest updates on my books.

Books By P.G.Van

Check out my Amazon page for the full list of books.